FIRST NIGHT RIDE

Sexy Stories Collection

VOLUME 33

10 EROTIC SHORT STORIES

KELLIE GRANIER

Publisher's Note: This is a work of fiction. Names,
characters, places, and incidents are a product of
the author's imagination. Locales and public
names are sometimes used for atmospheric
purposes. Any resemblance to actual people, living
or dead, or to businesses, companies, events,
institutions, or locales is completely coincidental.

First Night Ride/ Kellie Granier. -- 1st ed.
Xplicit Press, an imprint of TLM Media LLC

ISBN-13: 978-1-62327-564-8
ISBN-10: 1-62327-564-4
eISBN: 978-1-62327-612-6

Printed in the United States of America

CONTENTS

1 HONEY'S FIRST GANGBANG

Honey's lover unstrapped her wrists and pushed on her shoulder, forcing her down to her hands and knees. He used another spreader bar to secure her wrists there, strapping her in place. She had her back to the door, and she heard it whisper open but she couldn't see who was joining them. She knew better than to look around to satisfy her curiosity--when Dan wanted her to know, he would tell her. Until then, she stared at the floor in front of her, taking deep breaths while she waited for the next part of his lesson.

The review portion of the evening had been fun. She got to show her lover just how good she could be, got to swallow his cock even if he wouldn't let her swallow his cum. Her pussy was squishy wet, her thighs slick with her arousal, her muscles pulled tight while the blood rushed to her lower stomach. She ached in ways she couldn't begin to understand, as though every single nerve-ending had woken up and screamed at the same time. She hurt in areas she didn't remember ever feeling before. Worse, she'd never been so aware of her pussy or how badly she needed to be filled. At that point, she'd be thankful for anything, even a single finger, though she really wanted more than that. Dan wanted her to be patient, wanted her to learn and understand that it wasn't always about her needs, but at the moment, she literally couldn't think about anything else. Not even the stranger who was now standing in the room, watching her tremble while she waited for the next stage of her night.

He wasn't the only guest, either. The door opened again and again and again. She heard it each time, but it was impossible to know how many people came in. The thick carpet muffled their footsteps and she still wasn't allowed to turn her head to take stock of the situation. She automatically tried to squeeze her thighs together to relieve the throbbing ache there, but with her legs locked to the spreader bar she couldn't even do that. Her pussy was on full display, her shaved skin glistening under the low lights. A pair of legs passed within her field of vision, and then another and another. They were quietly circling her, watching her, admiring her. She kept her eyes downcast, though she was desperate to see who was there. Even if she didn't know the men, she could at least get a read on what they were thinking, on what they were looking for. They were obviously friends of her lover's, but why were they there? What did they plan to do?

Dan buried his hand in her hair, the familiar pull immediately settling her doubts and putting her mind to rest. No more questions, no more curiosity. It didn't matter who they were or why they were there. All that mattered was pleasing her lover and she would do whatever she had to do, anything within her power, and more to do that.

"Since you've been such a good girl, I decided to call a few of my friends over." He yanked her head back to look her in the eye. Desire immediately flooded her system--pure lust because even before he was her lover he was the most beautiful man she'd ever seen. Being on the receiving end of his intense looks was more addicting than anything else in the world. He knew full well what effect he had on her and he'd done everything in his power to emphasize those reactions, building on them until she was completely and utterly in his thrall. She didn't want to be anywhere else in the world. "It's time to turn that little pussy out."

She didn't quite understand but she didn't dare ask either. He saw the question flickering over her face and smiled. "It's time for your first gangbang, sweetheart. And I hope you're ready because I know how these guys fuck. They aren't gentle and it won't be over any time soon. I should know. I trained them."

Honey murmured her understanding, her pulse skipping and her heartbeat accelerating. It was all she could do to not start panting right then and there. This was more than just a reward. This was a fantasy she never spoke of, one she didn't even dare ask about.

"You've been trained all wrong," he once told her. "You need a new Lover. Somebody who understands you." She never realized until that moment how true his words were. Her training was systematic, methodic, and now she was going to reap the rewards she never expected.

"They all know your safe word," he added.

"Yes, Lover." She had absolutely no intention of using that word. No matter how far they pushed her, no matter how much they wanted to take from her, she was not going to use that word. Truth be told, she didn't want to have a word at all. She trusted her lover and she trusted him to know exactly how much she could take and where her boundaries were, but he insisted. At least for now, maybe after they had more time together and more training they could abandon the artificial constructs of control and she could submit to him entirely, with no option of backing out, of being anything but *his* to use, to love, to do with as he pleased.

She heard the men moving as they undressed, talking quietly to each other as they dropped their pants, kicked off their shoes, removed their shirts. She caught brief glimpses of them from the corners of her eyes and there seemed to be five in all. She also caught the occasional glimpse of their cocks, and every single one of them was at least as big as her lover, if not bigger. If they fucked like him, she was going to be in for one hell of a night. The thought made her drip with fresh arousal, and there was no doubt that she was completely ready for the first big dick.

"God, look at her, all wet and ready to go." One of them said.

"Shit yeah, you've trained her well, Sir."

"Thank you, but you can't train something like that. She's just a natural."

He wasn't complimenting her directly,

but the words still had a profound effect on her. Any praise at all was eagerly collected, gathered close, and held forever. She wasn't used to it, didn't even quite believe that he should recognize her existence, much less find reasons to praise her. Which was partially why she was so obsessed with pleasing him. Otherwise he might wake up one day and realize that he should be spending his time with somebody more worthy, more deserving, than her.

She felt the blunt tip of a cock press against her opening and then he was sliding inside, her pussy welcoming the intrusion with a series of flutters. She caught her breath and dropped her head down, her hair falling all around her, obscuring her vision. The cock moved deeper and deeper, stretching her tight hole.

She hadn't been fucked in over a week, and for the first time, she realized that was part of her lover's plan. He always had plans. Everything was intentional--there were no accidents in his world. Now she could see that he was intentionally not stretching her out, intentionally pushing her to the very brink and then leaving her aching and unsatisfied because it would be better this way. She couldn't move too much, but she still had the leverage to push her hips back and meet the intruding length. The man behind her groaned and shoved forward, claims the final few inches until he was balls deep.

A hand pushed through her tresses, shoving her hair away from her face and yanking her chin up. A thick cock with an angry red crown suddenly filled her vision and she automatically parted her lips, opening her mouth to accept him. He didn't waste any time, pushing until he reached the back of her throat. She relaxed her jaw and closed her lips around him, using the momentum of the cock pistoling in and out of her pussy to drive her onto the dick. He moved with hard thrusts, mercilessly fucking her face while the man behind her pounded into her pussy.

The orgasm Dan already allowed her actually made it more difficult to hold herself back. Her body was already primed, and she was naturally multi-orgasmic. With two thick dicks sawing in and out of her body, she didn't think she had a chance in hell. She mentally shrugged and resigned herself to the punishment. She didn't think Dan would call off the gangbang, which meant he would find other ways to make her pay in the long term. Well, Honey thought she could live with that. She always paid her debts, and that included the debts she accrued with too many unauthorized orgasms.

It happened without warning, the pleasure sweeping through her so intensely that she couldn't hold it back, couldn't resist the rising tide. She screamed around the dick in her mouth and he pushed forward even further, burying himself deep in her throat, silencing her. That didn't stop the climax, though. She was poised at the very peek, her body slamming back to meet each hard thrust, pussy clenching down so hard that the man groaned. "God, I can't..." His cock jerked within her and even though he was wearing a condom she knew he blew his load. How much time had passed? It seemed like hardly any time at all.

"My turn," the man above her head announced, pulling his dick free from her lips. He quickly settled in his new position behind her, fumbling a condom on within seconds, and pounding into her swollen pussy. She was puffy with desire, her flesh tender and bruised from the pounding she just received. The sensations were extremely intense as a result, and she felt a swell of desire and a sudden surge of power between her thighs. It was all she could do to keep herself still and not pound back. She wanted to take control with her hips, wanted to fuck herself back on the cock that been fucking her throat.

A new dick appeared in her line of sight and once again she automatically opened her mouth, not even waiting for the order. She accepted him as the throbbing shaft filled her pussy, stretching her in new ways.

He had no intention of going slow or tender. Didn't want to take his time or let her catch her breath. He moved like he was pounding into a living doll, a fuck hole that existed only for his pleasure. It was in the way he shuttled his cock, the way he touched her, the harsh grunts. She nearly melted from the heat of it, almost too distracted to do a good job with her mouth. But the man in front of her didn't really expect anything from her, either. Both of them wanted a warm hole to fuck, and nothing more. So she relaxed into the pounding without reservation, letting her body be pushed and pulled and moved and pummeled without a hint of resistance.

There was no pain. No matter what they did or how hard they used her, Honey was completely past the point of pain. Every sensation was processed as the purest of pleasures, every second pushing her closer and closer to another orgasm. Knowing that, these were complete strangers to her, that she was being watched and judged, and that all of this was only for Dan's pleasure set off another chain reaction of bliss. She wanted to fight it, but she couldn't. Her body clenched down, her fingers curling into fists, and her hips went off on their own thing, frantically slamming back, desperately moving harder and harder. The man behind her swore under his breath and then his cock was jerking so hard against her walls that he set her off on another orgasm, this one sweeping through her fast and hard, like a January blizzard.

The man behind her moved away, and the man with the dick in her mouth pulled free. They rotated, a new dick taking its place against her lips while the one she sucked on lined up with her dripping pussy. She risked a glance above to see if she could find her lover, but he was not standing anywhere nearby. He was probably directly behind her, his keen eyes taking in every single detail, making a note of every reaction--and probably every orgasm she didn't have permission for. She wanted to feel him so bad, but not as bad as she wanted to see him. Wanted to see approval or even appreciation on his face, though a part of her knew she hadn't done anything yet to earn his approval.

The third dick to claim her pussy was the biggest yet, and unlike the others, he couldn't take her in one easy stroke. He pushed the first inch in, working his way slowly even though by now she was stretched and wet. She was also well-fucked and swollen, her pussy gripped him even more tightly as he gained inch after inch. She forced her hips to remain still, her back to remain straight, forced herself to take his dick on his terms. It was hard to remember sometimes that the ability to do something didn't translate into the right to do something. Another lesson Dan was doing his best to teach her. Her frame trembled and she had to blink her eyes rapidly to get rid of the sting of sweat and the sudden spots dancing before her vision. Her body was a vessel empty of everything, ready to be filled again and again and again.

The pounding she receiving was exactly as hard as she expected, and her body responded with absolute glee. So much so that she once again lost track of herself. She forgot she was supposed to be the fuck hole, and went crazy on the man's cock, fucking herself as hard and as fast as she could manage with her legs in the spreader bar and her mouth occupied with the fourth cock of the day. Sweat gathered at the back of her neck and rolled down her ribs and she could feel her hair sticking to the top of her scalp. Her nostrils flared as she struggled to get enough oxygen in her burning lungs and exhausted limbs, though it was hard to really catch her breath with a big shaft blocking her air passage. She didn't need it, though. She could survive; she learned how to survive on less air. Lover was preparing her for breath play.

Once again, she triggered the man inside of her into a surprise orgasm, her muscles fluttering and clamping around his dick, her hips bucking and her spine twisting and arching. She moved like a wild animal. She felt like a wild animal, a being completely incapable of self-control or higher thoughts. She was in her most animal, primal state, and she was sad that she was already half-way through all the cocks in the room. Didn't Dan say they were supposed to last a long time? Weren't they trained by him to be the best? She had a feeling she was supposed to be the exhausted one; instead she was raring to go, impatient and annoyed by every single second she had to wait for the next dick to split her pussy open.

"Should have warned us about this one," one of them laughed. "She's making short work of us."

"We're just putting her through her paces," Dan promised. "Can't break this one without some time and patience. That doesn't mean we won't break her at all."

Honey's head spun with the promise she heard in her lover's silky voice. Maybe she wasn't doing anything wrong. Maybe he wanted her to wear herself out, to steal as many orgasms as she could before he took control again. If that was the case, she wasn't going to waste this opportunity. She turned her attention to the dick in her mouth with new vigor, sucking on it hungrily; intent on tasting somebody's cum before the day was finished.

She buried her nose in the wiry curls at the base and flexed her throat around the crown, swallowing again and again around the swollen flesh. She could feel the vein on the underside throbbing, and taste the vague hint of salt at the back of her throat. A hand cupped the back of her skull, holding her in place, while his hips moved faster and faster, as if they were actually on pistons. He brutally fucked her throat, his dick even bigger than Dan's, bruising the tender muscles behind her tongue, his balls hitting her chin. She felt them tighten, and she did what she could to pull away slightly, putting the tip of his cock closer to her tongue so she could taste it when he finally burst. His cock jerked and then painted the back of her tongue, tasting even better than she thought it would.

"I can see what you mean about breaking this one," he said as he pulled his half-hard cock from her lips. "She's good at what she does but she doesn't really get what her role is, does she?"

"No, not quite. But she will. Come on,

let's get a beer."

And just like that, she was alone once again, with his promise still ringing in her ears. Breaking her...learning her role...her position...her place. She shivered in the aftermath of her pleasure, not sure what to think. She wasn't going to change, and even though she wanted nothing more than to submit to Dan, she wasn't going to break, either...

2 SILVER TEQUILA AND VEGAS LIGHTS

The debate began the second they saw her at the club, and continued long after the three of them brought the party up to the suite. If she wasn't Jennifer Love Hewett, she was the woman's long lost twin sister. She introduced herself as Annie, but that didn't mean anything. Nobody used their real name in Vegas ... or maybe that was the only place a person could use their real name. Either way, Annie had the same heart-shaped face, the same pouty lips, and the same beautiful tits and rocking body as the well-known actress. She was like a dream come to life, something spun from the threads of his favorite fantasies.

There were still several full bottles from their pre-party festivities, and Nick tracked down a bottle of each rum and tequila while Alex settled with their lovely new friend on the couch in front of the huge picture window. From their vantage, they could see not only the frantic, beautiful glow of the Strip, but all of Vegas laid out in a far-reaching grid, encroaching ever deeper into the darkness of the desert. He found a good station on the satellite radio and joined them on the couch, sitting as close to her left side as Alex sat to her right, offering her a shot glass. She accepted it like she accepted all of the other drinks offered to her that evening with a grateful smile and a quick toss of her head, downing the full contents.

"Nice. 1800 Silver?"

"How did you know?"

"I know my tequila."

She held her shot glass out, silently requesting a refill. Nick was more than happy to oblige, filling it to the brim and grinning as she threw that one down, too. She tossed the shot glass away without a second glance and smiled at him, his dick twitching at the sly curve of her lips. She ran her tongue over the pink skin to collect the remaining drops of tequila, then gathered her long hair into her fist and pulled it from the back of her neck.

"Would you mind rubbing my neck?" She shot a smile over her shoulder to Alex. "I'm so tense. It's been such a long week."

Nick watched Alex's fingers, the color of dark wheat, glide over her milky-white skin, smoothing the tips over the narrow ridges of her shoulders to cradle the delicate column of her throat. She moaned slightly as he pushed his thumbs into her tense flesh, her earrings jingling and catching the light as she dropped her head forward. Alex caught Nick's eye over her bowed head and grinned, the gleam in his eye saying everything. The deal was closed. Now it was time to act.

Nick took her by the hand, folding her fingers around his left hand while he worked his right up and down her arm. He pressed his thumb to her pulse, smiling as it quickened in response to Alex's touch. He leaned forward, blowing a cool stream of air over the nape of her neck. Goosebumps rolled down her arms as Nick brought her wrist to his lips, barely skimming over her thin skin. She sucked her breath in sharply, and her pulse felt like a hummingbird fluttering against his mouth. He left a trail of light kisses up her arm, taking a deep breath as he reached her shoulder. He loved the smell of her perfume and her musk, the combination making him heady, making his mouth dry.

She took him by surprise, sliding her

fingers through his hair to cut the back of his head and pulling him close. She paused just before their mouths met, and he hung over her lips, lost in her scent. Alex found a sensitive spot and she gasped, her beautiful lips parting, a hint of tequila and sweet fruit washing over him just before she dragged him down. His tongue dove into her hot mouth. He wanted to taste the tequila on her tongue, wanted to drown in her. He sensed movement, but didn't realize what was happening until she shifted beneath him, sliding between Alex's legs and leaning back to rest on his chest. Nick followed her down without breaking the kiss, his chest pressed to hers, her cute little dress pulled high up her thighs.

She broke the kiss first, tilting her head back to seek Alex's lips. Nick couldn't resist the temptation of her throat, and he kissed down the column until he reached the sweet-smelling skin over her pulse. The sound of the two of them kissing sent darts of heat to his groin, and his cock throbbed against the confines of his jeans. His fingers shook as he pulled at his pants, freeing his heavy erection from its cage. Alex's hands slipped into view as he pulled at the bodice of her dress, forcing it down her bust. Her pert titties bounced free of the material, providing two perfect, pink targets for his mouth. He dove to catch one between his lips, sucking the flesh into a hard nub against his teeth. She moaned, and this sound was unlike the others. This was meant for him alone.

He lifted his head long enough to snag the bottle of tequila from the floor. He poured a healthy amount over her chest and tits, following the flow of booze with his mouth, lapping it from her taut skin. She moved against his tongue, her lithe body twisting and shivering as the chilled tequila dripped into the valley between her breasts. He chased it with his hot tongue, following the curve of her flesh. A perfect drop of the clear liquid rested on her pink nipple, like dew on a rose petal, and he caught it with his tongue, flicking it again and again over her soft skin.

Nick looked up, watching through his lashes as Alex and Annie devoured each other's mouths. They were a stunning pair, easily stealing his breath from his lungs. He needed more, his whole body heavy with his desire. Energy sparked between them like static electricity, shocking him every time skin moved against skin. The sparks erupted into a full firestorm when two hands, one big, one small, gripped him by the hair and pushed him down, down, down to the cradle between her thighs.

He hooked his fingers around the black lace of her thong and tugged gently. She immediately lifted her hips, allowing him to tug the panties down her thighs. He guided her foot through the hole, and then let the material dangle from the toe of her stiletto. She settled lower against Alex, hooking one leg over the back of the couch so he could see her smooth mound with its delicate pink lips and the tip of her clit peeking up like a pearl.

Alex's large hand on the back of his head pushed him into her sweet flesh. He went in with his tongue out, seeking her swollen clit, smiling as she whimpered and wiggled against him, her hips jerking and rolling in time with his tongue. Her other leg went over his shoulder, her heel digging into his back as she lifted herself higher, grinding against his mouth and chin. Once again, he sensed movement, and when her hand guided him lower, to where Alex's cock bobbed free of his pants, he obediently sucked the head into his mouth.

He tasted of salty pre-come and sweat, but Nick's nose was still full of the scent of her arousal, and it still coated the back of his tongue. She shifted again, moving so her pussy lips covered his shaft, spreading her juices over his flesh. Nick's nose pushed into her flesh, and his tongue traveled from Alex's tight dick skin to her silky smooth pussy. He burrowed in closer, letting his nose grind against her clit as he feasted on both, his breath still hot with tequila against their slick flesh.

He wanted more of her. He wanted to lick the very source of her sweet juice. He fisted Alex's cock, holding it out of the way while his tongue slithered forward to her tight opening. He wiggled his tongue against the tight ring, pushing it deeper and deeper into her tight channel. For a moment, he had complete control of both of them, his tongue working in and out of her cunt while he pumped Alex's wooden erection. His balls felt heavy, his entire groin throbbing for something hot and tight, something that would wrap around his flesh and ease the maddening pulse.

He dragged his tongue back up her slit to find her clit again, sucking on it until her moans turned into ragged screams. By then, he couldn't stand the tightness of his clothes for another second. He felt like he was going to crawl out of his skin, and as much as he didn't want to, he had to pull himself away long enough to wiggle out of his clothes. As soon as he stood, he caught Alex's eyes and a silent message passed between them. She looked like a lamb caught in the clutches of a big bear as he held her tightly and slid lower on the large sofa. A roll of his hips and a small nudge, and Alex was inside of her tight, wet body, watching Nick with heavy eyes while he quickly undressed.

Nick carefully lowered himself to the couch, resting on one knee and stretching himself over their breathless, sleek bodies. He claimed her mouth, let her drink deeply on the taste of her own arousal, and then attacked Alex's mouth, kissing him with the full force of his soaring passion. Their tongues dueled; Alex's invading Nick's mouth as he pumped his hips into Annie's welcoming body.

"You should be inside of her," Alex whispered. "Want to feel you, too."

Nick moved from his lips, kissing down Alex's chin and throat and chest. His hair tickled Nick's mouth, and with his nose pressed against Alex's chest, he finally smelled past his expensive cologne, his body spray, to his natural musk. A few inches lower, and his mouth was on her smooth skin, nestled in her sweeter curves. She caught his jaw and drew him to her mouth, her tongue slipping out to meet his. His sensitive crown slid between her lips, pressing against her engorged clit. Then he slid lower, to where her body met Alex's.

At first, he wasn't sure he could do it. She lay quivering between the two of them, shifting her hips and mewling with impatience as he considered his options. Alex looked at him with intense, heavy-lidded eyes, waiting for him to do as he was told. He cupped his balls, giving them a squeeze and a gentle tug, trying to ease the ache there. He already felt like he was two seconds from exploding, he wasn't sure how he was going to handle the extra sweet tightness of her pussy with Alex's cock buried inside.

He used that cock to guide him into her swollen flesh, sliding against his throbbing erection to finally bury himself in her surprisingly elastic pussy. He'd been in some tight pieces before, but this went beyond simple tightness. This was heat more intense than the sun. This was the endless throbbing of flesh and three thundering heartbeats crashing into one endless sound, one endless sensation. She wrapped her arms around him and there wasn't an inch of light or space between them. They were all three connected, energy spilling from vessel to vessel, like air exhaled and then snatched into new lungs.

She tried to stay quiet at first, pressing her mouth to Nick's every time a shout threatened to erupt. But soon enough she was thrashing around and breathless, her shouts loud explosions over their more quiet, but frantic pants. He reached between their bodies to find her clit, and he pressed down on the hard nub as he drove his hips forward, burying himself as deeply as he could. Alex moved then, sliding out, pressing in, and then Nick moved. They took turns like that, both holding themselves perfectly, painfully still when they filled her at the same time, then sliding their hips back and forth, so she could feel both dicks at once.

Nick was getting close to blowing his load when he felt small hands press against his chest. Frowning, he paused, and then realized she wanted him to move back. He pulled out of her and she increased the pressure of her hands, forcing him all the way to his back. She took the opportunity to rise from Alex's lap and shimmy out of her dress, allowing his eyes to feast on every perfect inch of her.

"Both of you, on your back. You, slide lower. Yes, like that." She gripped their cocks, holding their shafts together, stroking the thick flesh with both palms. She lowered her head, lavishing attention on both dicks with her eager tongue, lapping up the taste of her arousal and their pre-come, still leaking freely from their tips.

She straddled their legs, her pussy

gliding over their cockheads. Nick could feel Alex's pounding pulse, and the heat of her flesh licking at him like flames dancing over kindling. He couldn't look away as she sank down over both of them, moving lower and lower. Alex wrapped his hands around her trim waist, and Nick entwined his fingers through hers, supporting her weight as she leaned forward to take the final inches of their shafts. Her fingers locked around his once she was fully seated, and she used her hold to lift herself up a few inches. She shifted down again and both men gasped, the friction of their bodies connecting overwhelming the heat.

She rose like a goddess out of the water; her head flung back, her tits arched forward, the neon lights painting her skin red, blue, and green. There was no doubt that she was in charge then. If she was a Goddess, they were her eager acolytes, worshipping her curves and her lines and her light. Alex's hands traveled up and down her ribs, cupped her breasts, let her perky nipples peak through the bars of his fingers. He pulled and teased them, and each twitch and flick of his fingers made her clench around them, bearing down with intense strength.

Nick brought his hand to her pussy without releasing her fingers, using his thumb to seek out her clit. She shouted and jerked her hips, hard, bucking with enough force to make Nick's eyes cross. Alex whimpered, and he never heard anything like that from his friend. It was a low, nearly broken, absolutely helpless sound, and then his hold on her tightened and she bucked her hips and screamed, but this time, she didn't stop moving. She found her rhythm, and they followed her, their hips working in silent accordance, following a natural beat that had them sliding against each other in the most maddening, delicious way. He'd had threesomes before, but none like this, and he had to admit, it made a huge difference. There was no barrier between their dicks, nothing blocking him from feeling Alex's heat, or his pulse, or the perfect texture of his skin.

The quality of her moans changed, and she clenched tighter than ever before, her spine lengthening as a series of explosions went off beneath her skin. She quaked, her muscles convulsing and fluttering, her walls swelling around their thick dicks. Nick tried to put a hand up to slow her, but she refused to stop, her clit grinding against his hand, jerking and twitching like his cock. She was impossible to subdue, couldn't be stopped or controlled. Her body was a force of nature going off around them and over them. Somehow, he even felt her inside of him, as though her pleasure kindled fresh sparks at the base of his spine.

He didn't want to come too quickly but the very thought of it was nearly his undoing. All he could imagine was his wad painting Alex's dick as he pumped her full of his come. The sight of it clinging to his dark skin, white and salty and sticky, pushed him all too close to the edge. He fought it, though, dragging his mind away from anything remotely dangerous. He might be able to control his thoughts, but he couldn't control the sensations buffeting him, becoming more and more intense by the second. He might have been able to tolerate it, but her pussy was so damned tight, and Alex's cock was so damned thick, and touching her was like touching a wildfire. Fucking her was almost like throwing himself into the volcano, and once he took that swan dive, how would he ever pull himself back out?

She couldn't pull herself back from the heat. Her orgasms slammed through her, one after the other, each with bone-shaking intensity. She'd ride one out only to be hit again, her explosions of pleasure forming a long chain that wrapped around the three of them in tighter and tighter circles. His chest constricted, forcing him to gasp faster and faster for the necessary oxygen, and then it was out of his hands. His breath lodged in his throat, and everything inside of him shattered at once, the force of his pleasure simply breaking him apart as his cock jerked again and again, slicking her walls and his dick.

He was still mostly hard, almost trapped inside of her, and his fresh come only reduced the friction, allowing her to move even faster. She went crazy, pounding down on their dicks, pummeling him with the force of her desire. Nick had no idea how Alex was holding up against this, but he was awash in an ocean of bliss, and it kept carrying him farther and farther from the shoreline. He could almost see himself back on the horizon, losing definition, becoming smaller and smaller and smaller.

He felt a hand seeking out his, and realized it was Alex. He fumbled free of her grip and closed his fingers around Alex's, gripping him with as much force as he had in his exhausted, almost sated body. Alex gripped him back and a red and gold energy suddenly flared through him, igniting his nerve-endings and warming his blood. He felt in control again and his cock hardened, his blood rushing south while his heart beat out a new, harsher rhythm. Don't give up on me now, Alex seemed to be saying.

Alex pushed her forward, urging her to bend at the waist and press her tits against Nick's chest. Somehow, without pulling free of her pussy, Alex followed, getting his knees under him and laying out across her back. Nick looked up, blinking while the ceiling spun around their heads, stunned by the full force of the beauty staring down at him. He needed to kiss somebody, needed to feel soft lips and hot breath, and he pointed his chin in invitation, waiting for one of them to make the claim. Alex acted first, leaning over his shoulder to sear his mark against Nick's lips, his tongue invading Nick's pliant mouth.

Alex began to move then, driving his large body forward with powerful thrusts of his hips. He was in complete control, leaving Nick and Annie with no choice but to hold on for the ride, each of them grunting each time Alex slammed his thick dick into her stretched pussy. He held Nick's ankles and forced them up over his head, leaning forward even further, pushing until his balls brushed against Nick's sac. Annie tried to brace herself with her hands on Nick's shoulders, but it wasn't long until she gave up, sagging against Nick with her head tucked against his neck while Alex pounded into her. Their balls slapped together and the relentless friction of his shaft sliding over

Nick's all-too-sensitive dick was nearly his undoing.

He'd lost track of Annie's orgasms. They were impossible to count, especially now that they were virtually indistinguishable. Every few seconds he would feel her entire body prepare itself, clench, remain stark and tense and frozen and then her whole frame would shake with the force of the latest explosion. She was drenching them now, soaking them with her come every time Alex pushed her into another orgasm, and Nick thought he could be intoxicated from the smell, drunk with the sweet scent of it.

He broke free of Alex's mouth to be swept up in by her smaller tongue, losing himself in the kiss before he even had the chance to catch his breath. He fisted her hair, holding it tightly against her scalp, shivering with delight as she moaned into the kiss. He gave it a hard yank, sending her rushing to a new climax, her hips jerking with wild abandon, her thighs and lips trembling. She sobbed against his mouth, her fingers curling into tiny fists that rained down on his shoulders and back without malice. The third time she punched the firm muscles on his shoulders, her hands flattened against the skin and he felt the sting of ten nails sinking into his flesh. The pain was a new sensation to sharpen the edge of his pleasure, and he caught her hands, holding them down, pressing her crescent nails even deeper, and forming ten bloody moons across his shoulders.

Alex roared then, his back arching as he pushed his cock as deep into her as he could, filling her with his seed. The splash and slippery texture of his come coating everything sent Nick on another spiral of pleasure, and he could only clutch them both as close as possible as he emptied his balls a second time.

When they finally collapsed into an unmoving pile of limbs, they were all completely slick with sweat, wet from head to toe. The combined smell of their sex and sweat made something stir deep in his stomach, but he was too tired to get hard again. The two men were more or less still, only their chests moving as they struggled to catch their breath, but she kept wiggling against them, sighing and shaking every time an aftershock raced down her spine.

They only disentangled themselves when Alex suggested they move the party to the suite's king size bed, and Nick was surprised they could all make it that far without collapsing. They fell together with kisses, booze in hand, tequila like fire burning through their veins.

3 NO GUTS NO GLORY

Art never let anything distract him from his ride--not even the presence of a certain Leo Knight--until after that buzzer sounded and his score was officially in the books. He hated to lose, and he approached every event with the same single-minded determination that carried him all the way to the PBR World Finals the previous year. He planned to make another appearance in Las Vegas that October, and every ride counted. But after he tied himself to a behemoth for eight seconds, he could devote as much time as he liked to the topic of Leo Knight.

Leo had been riding bulls for as long as Art. They busted their professional cherries at the same event, and Leo had been dogging Art's heels ever since. No matter how much Art dominated in the rankings, Leo was always right fucking there. He never gave Art any room for mistakes--all it took was one bad night for him and one good ride for Leo, and their rankings would flip. Leo was the enemy, his greatest rival, and the one person Art should keep his distance from. What's the problem with that? Leo was too goddamned nice, too goddamned decent, and way too...handsome. He was tall-- taller than anybody else on the circuit-- and he stood out in a sport dominated by short, stocky men with his bright red hair and his ready smile. Art always noticed him, his attention drawn to his lanky gait and his long frame and once eye contact was made, everything else was lost.

Even if Art resolved to keep his distance, Leo would never let him. Once the rides were done, all the cowboys paired off or formed small groups, gossiping about each other, talking about their rides, making predictions for the next night, waiting for their wives or their girlfriends to pick them up, and in the chaos, Leo found him. Leo always found him, and Art always gave in to the attraction he felt. Something about Leo drew him back again and again, and Art had long ago given up on explaining it. He didn't understand what this ginger-headed, lanky smiling son of a bitch had over him, or why he couldn't ignore the pull between them. Ultimately, he was just grateful that Leo felt it, too, because Art didn't really do pining.

"Hey. Nice ride." Leo held his hand out, his bright, genuine smile supporting his compliment. "That was something else. I thought for sure Yellow Sky would get one over on you, but you proved me wrong."

"God hasn't made a beast I can't ride," Art announced.

"I wouldn't speak too soon. You know you could draw Misty Waters tomorrow."

Art snorted. "And with a name like Misty Waters I'm shaking in my boots."

"You know nobody's ridden ol' Misty in about two years, right? He takes down every cowboy he meets."

"He hasn't met me yet." Art knew he sounded cocky, but he was on a streak. He was deep into that mystical realm known as The Zone, where every ride went his way and nothing could stop him. Not even a mean old gray bull with a white face that was known to trample the riders he tossed from his back. "Can I buy you a beer?"

"Actually, I got a thirty rack back at my trailer. Was wondering if you wanted to help me finish them off."

Art beamed and slapped his friend on the back. "That's why you're the idea man. What about Will and Gillie? Want to call them over?"

"Oh, I already talked to them and Will's girl is in town. I guess she has a week off from school and she brought a friend."

"They could join us."

"It sounds like they have plans," Leo said dismissively. "But that doesn't mean we can't enjoy ourselves, right?"

"Absolutely."

Art followed Leo back to his trailer, carrying his chaps and his hat over one arm, his spurs jingling with each step. He nodded at the men he knew as they passed by, smiled at the girls he didn't know, and tried to avoid the fans that waving pictures and cameras, seeking autographs and photos with their favorite riders. Usually, he was happy to indulge them, but Leo's cold beers were calling out to him, and he just wanted to crack a cold one and put his feet up.

And maybe a small part of him just wanted to be alone with Leo. Sure, he suggested calling Will and Gillie, but he was more than a little relieved that they had plans. Being alone with Leo often felt like a good idea in theory--until it actually happened and he realized he was ALONE with Leo, and his nerves went haywire and his brain short-circuited and everything felt dizzy and confused and all wrong. When that happened, he couldn't call Will or Gillie fast enough. God, why did Leo always make him think of things he didn't want to think about? Why did Leo make him feel the things he felt?

Art shut and locked the trailer door behind him, tossing his things on the Formica dining table. Leo had been one of the top riders for years, and though he wasn't an ostentatious sort, he did like living and traveling with a certain level of luxury. Art was grateful for that now, happy to sink into the RV's plush couch with a cold beer in one hand and a leftover slice of pizza in the other.

"You really were amazing tonight," Leo said, sitting beside him. Almost close enough to touch him. Almost, but not quite.

"Thanks."

"Sometimes watching you...it makes me wonder what the hell I'm doing out there."

Art laughed. "What do you mean?"

"I mean, I don't think I can beat you. And honestly...I don't want to."

Art grimaced and winced at once. "Don't talk like that. Of course you want to beat me. I mean, if I was the only thing standing between you and a twenty-five thousand dollar purse, you'd tear right through me, wouldn't you?"

"I guess."

"And I'd tear through you," Art said comfortably. "We know where our priorities are."

"Yeah. Still, Art...I've been doing this for a lot of years, and I've never seen anybody like you. It's like...you have some sort of connection with the bulls. Like you know what they're going to do before they do it."

"Sometimes I do," Art admitted. "I don't really know how...I mean, I can usually sense which way a bull is going to jump or if he's going to kick or spin or slam his head back. But sometimes...I just know." He shrugged. "It's hard to explain."

"Whatever it is, it's made you the best. And it's been an honor knowing you and riding with you."

Art felt himself blush and he shifted uncomfortably, taking a long, cold drink from the can. Leo wouldn't look away from him, and Art found it difficult to meet his gaze. "You don't need to talk like this is a funeral. I'm not going anywhere, and last I checked, neither were you."

"I'm thinking about retiring."

"What? Why? You can't."

"I'm getting a bit long in the tooth for this, Art. I think it's best to quit while I'm ahead of the game...before I get really hurt. Don't you?"

"What are you going to do instead?"

"My dad has plenty of use for me on the ranch. Maybe work there, find a nice girl, and settle down. Have a normal life."

Art wrinkled his nose. "That's sounds boring." In fact, it sounded exactly like the life Art wanted to avoid. The very life he fled from when he climbed onto the back of his first bull.

"There's nothing wrong with boring. Boring can be good. Great, in fact."

"Boring can be good? What's going on with you? You almost sound like you've been...spooked. Has something happened?" Did he have a bad ride? Did something get under his skin?

"No, nothing's happened. Nothing like you thinks, anyway. It's just...a good time to be considering a change."

Art shook his head. "Yeah, I don't believe that horseshit. There's something going on here. You might as well come clean. I can't help you if you don't talk."

"What makes you think I want your help?"

"We're buddies. You're entitled to my help whether you want it or not."

"I don't know if I can talk about it with you, Art. It's...complicated."

"I like complicated and you still have plenty of beers. So spill it. Besides, how complicated can it be really? Do you owe somebody money?"

"No."

"Been fucking somebody's wife?"

"No."

"Somebody's girlfriend?"

Leo shook his head. "No. That's partially the problem."

"You're not getting laid? Seriously? Because there are about a dozen girls out there waiting to get your autograph who would be happy to come back to your trailer for a little somethin'-somethin'."

"I know, but...I don't want them. See, Art, I'm not really into the girls out there."

"Because, they're wearing buckle bunnies?"

"Because they're girls," Leo said softly.

"Because...oh. Oh. Well...I think you have some fanboys, too. But...maybe you have somebody specific in mind?"

"Yeah, maybe I do." Leo's voice was laced with sadness and...regret?...and he slowly brought his beer to his mouth. He drank it down without pause, crushing the empty can in one huge hand and reaching for another. Leo didn't look at him when he said it, and Art had no real reason to think this but he had the sense that maybe...maybe...Leo was referring to him.

The thought stunned him into silence, and for several long minutes, they were both wrapped up in their own thoughts. To be honest, Art had never, ever considered being with another man, and he was sure that even if he liked dudes, Leo wouldn't be his type. He was too big, his hands like paws, his frame towering over Art's. Art thought he might like his men more petite. On the other hand, in three years of riding, he'd never met anybody who commanded his attention and his affection the way Leo did. Hell, he didn't even give anybody else a passing thought when he and Leo were at the same event. Not even to the girls who would have been more than happy to give it up to him. He'd never kissed another dude, so who was to say he didn't like it? There was only one way to know for sure, right?

Finishing his second beer, he tossed the can away indifferently and turned to Leo, who was staring into the distance with a defeated look on his face. His strawberry blond beard was a little off-putting, but his pink lips were even more alluring. Art took a deep breath, feeling like he was about to climb on the biggest, baddest, orneriest, rottenest bulls in existence. His stomach climbed into his throat--a familiar sensation that he learned to ignore long ago. His palms were sweaty and his mouth was dry, and his heart thudded in his ears, pushing and prodding him forward, further and further until he crossed the line and stepped into the land of no return.

"Art...what?"

"Shh," Art breathed his lips less than an inch from Leo's. "I just want to see..."

"Don't if--"

But Art cut off his words with a hard kiss that didn't betray his sudden surge of nerves and doubt. What if Leo really didn't want this? What if he, himself, really didn't want this? It seemed like the negative consequences might outweigh any good he thought he might accomplish, but he committed himself to a course of action and he'd be damned if was going to turn yellow now. So he kissed Leo with authority, plunging his tongue into Leo's mouth, holding him in place so he could explore the curves and hollows of his hot mouth. He ignored the alien sensation of whiskers against his lip and chin, focusing on the way Leo's lips fit over his, and the confident, intoxicating way he returned each of Art's caresses.

When he felt like his lungs might burst, Art lifted his head to meet Leo's wide, surprised gaze. They stared at each other for a long beat, Art's heart pounding and his dick throbbing. Yes, his dick was definitely hard--maybe not fully erect, but obviously very interested. Was this why he longed to be in Leo's presence? Had he constantly misunderstood his interest in the taller cowboy? That seemed very likely, because there was no mistaking the pleasure and desire coursing through him without a single drop of disgust or horror.

"Art..."

"Yes?"

"I think we ought to do that again."

"Yes," Art breathed just before their

mouths crashed together once again and Leo's long fingers began exploring Art's body. He moved up and down Art's arms and then over his torso, testing the hard, defined muscles before working on the buttons keeping his shirt in place. He cleared them away quickly and pushed the material down Art's shoulders. He shrugged the shirt away, too caught up in the kiss to be embarrassed by Leo's frantic search for his skin. He shivered at the first brush of skin-to-skin contact, that shiver turning into a full shudder as Leo broke away from Art's mouth to kiss a wet trail down his chest.

Art was used to being in charge when it came to situations like this, but now that Leo had the permission he was waiting for, he took full reign, pushing Art against the back of his couch and holding him there with one hand over his heart. Art knew his rapid heartbeat and racing pulse were undeniable tells, and his pulse only raced faster when he felt the tickle of Leo's lips over the sensitive point. He moved lower and lower, his beard so much softer than Art expected as Leo's mouth roamed over his well-developed pecs. Art watched him, fascinated, unsure of what to do with his hands as Leo feasted on him, mouth traveling further and further south. He tickled over Art's abs and blew a soft stream of breath over Art's hip and that startled Art out of his hazy lust.

"Wait..."

Leo looked up expectantly, his chin just an inch from Art's very obvious bulge. In that moment, Art saw everything Leo never showed him before--his hunger and his need, his eagerness to please, his lust. It was all stamped in his heated look, obvious on every inch of his face. Art's cock was so hard he didn't have the ability to think straight--all of the blood had rushed south so fast it left him dizzy. And God, his jeans hurt. He wasn't a small guy, and the zipper felt like it might cut right through his engorged cock.

"Yes?"

Art shook his head and gestured at his pants--please, please continue. Leo inclined his head, getting the message loud and clear, and tugged the zipper down. Art caught his breath as the zipper slowly exposed his hard-on, his eyes fluttering shut as Leo finally feasted his gaze on Art's flesh. He didn't want to see Leo looking at him, didn't need to see the interplay of emotion and lust on his face and in his eyes. Somehow, he expected Leo to study him for long minutes, but within seconds of freeing Art, he had his mouth around his dick.

Art sighed, sinking deeper into the couch, unconsciously sliding his ass closer to the edge. Leo continued to tug at

Art's pants without separating his mouth from the throbbing flesh, working the tight Levis down his thighs to his boots. He tugged them off and yanked everything away at once, leaving Art's legs bare and free. He immediately pulled Art's legs over his shoulders and sank beneath the weight of his limbs, lowering his mouth all the way to the base of Art's cock. Art groaned, lifting his hips, completely lost in the tight, wet heat. Leo's mouth was unbelievably soft, his tongue gentle and teasing and enticing. When Art reached his throat, he swallowed him down without hesitation, holding him in the soft, warm tunnel, swallowing around him until Art thought he might lose his head.

Leo cradled Art's balls in his palm, gently massaging them with his long fingers. Fingers that could wrap so tight around a leather rope those two thousand pounds of furious bull couldn't send him flying. Art knew first hand that those fingers could break him with endless pain, but instead they moved over his body like he was a skittish colt. No touch lingered to long, and the gentle massaging of his balls only goaded him closer to his orgasm.

He lost all sense of time and place, like the power of Leo's mouth was to pull him into an alternate dimension, where nothing but pleasure existed. He could not remember the last time he received a blowjob that was quite so...thorough. And thorough really was the best word for it. Leo lavished every inch with attention, used his entire mouth to explore and his entire body to power his thrusts. His long hair fell around him in a shield of burnished curls, and Art couldn't resist the temptation to gather up those locks in a tight fist. When he pulled Leo's hair away from his face, he saw something completely new--Leo's face set in an expression of perfect bliss. He responded readily to the tug on his hair, content to follow Art's lead as long as he didn't pull Leo's mouth completely free of his cock.

Art rose up, slamming Leo's face down to meet him with a brutal stroke. Leo grunted, but he seemed game, his hands spreading over Art's thighs, thumbs working into the gutters. He gagged and choked around Art's cock, the sound only driving him to pump his hips harder. His moans and grunts vibrated through Art's flesh, right to the base of his spine, which tingled in response. He was so close...and he tried to resist...tried so hard...but this was momentum that couldn't be denied. The rush of pleasure was the exact same rush he experienced when he heard that buzzer, when he knew he had his ride and would live to try again another day.

It was a rush that sex never, ever gave him before. Maybe if it had, he never would have found himself with an obsession that drove him all the way to the professional ranks.

"Oh fuck, oh my god, Leo, god, Leo, oh fuck..." He forced himself to stop talking, biting down and trying to communicate everything with his sated, dopey smile. He watched as Leo wiped his mouth but realized that he must have swallowed down Art's full load. His cock hung limply against his thigh, and he wondered if Leo just ruined blowjobs forever.

"That was so good," Art said thickly.

Leo cracked a beer open and took a long swallow. When he pulled the can away, Art couldn't help himself. He launched himself at Leo's mouth, his tongue probing deep past his lips, seeking out the bitterness of beer and the salty hint of Art himself. Leo closed his arms around him, holding with a bear's strength

4 GUTS AND GLORY

Leo cracked a beer open and took a long swallow. When he pulled the can away, Art couldn't help himself. He launched himself at Leo's mouth, his tongue probing deep past his lips, seeking out the bitterness of beer and the salty hint of Art himself. Leo closed his arms around him, holding with a bear's strength while their tongues danced together. Art's cock was already stirring again, a reaction he didn't expect. But then again, he didn't expect any of this, ever. He didn't know what was affecting him the most, but maybe it was as simple as Leo's hunger for him. It was in everything he did, in every touch and kiss, and Art couldn't believe he was standing there, locked in his best friend's arms, tasting his own cum on the man's tongue. Outside the trailer door was a world that wouldn't understand and maybe once that would have bothered Art, but now he couldn't bring himself to care.

Leo's hard cock was pressed to his hip, and Art moved his hand down, cupping the bulge and giving him a good squeeze. Leo gasped against his mouth, made some noise about how Art didn't have to do anything he didn't want to do, which Art promptly silenced with a bruising kiss. He wasn't doing anything he didn't want to do; he couldn't think of anything he wanted more. He bit down on Leo's bottom lip and chuckled at Leo's moan, nearly giddy with the possibilities. He never had this kind of experience. Surely he could sleep with girls every night, and he used to do his best to accomplish that very thing, but there was never any...fun. They fucked, they got the job done, and yeah, everybody got off. But Art never smiled like this, couldn't remember the last time this sense of joy and adventure colored every action and response.

He pulled open Leo's fly with a casual gesture, his fingers popping the button and then grasping the zipper. The sound was loud in the otherwise quiet trailer and his cock jerked, as if to say "Are you really doing this?" and yes, yes he really was. He yanked the jeans down and reached under the waistband of his tighty-whities, pushing them off his hips and freeing his cock.

"The carpets match the drapes I see," Art said with a twist of his lips, his attention locked on the full, vibrant red bush of air surrounding his shaft.

"Was there ever any doubt?"

Art snorted. "I guess not." Then they were kissing again because there were too many words, and Art was done with talking. All he wanted was to feel Leo's teeth against his lips and his tongue wiggling and darting around. He fisted Leo's long, thin cock, stroking the shaft like he liked his own shaft to be touched. It felt the same but completely different. The skin was just as smooth, satin over a core of iron, and the tip was glazed with pre-cum. He was a little longer than Art, but a little thinner. Maybe it wouldn't hurt too much. The more he stroked Leo, the more convinced he became that it wouldn't be so bad to feel it in his ass. Would Leo want to do that? Did he really want Leo to do that?

Art pushed the thought away. He could worry about that later. In the mean time, he wanted to at least return his amazing orgasm. Leo deserved at least that much from him. But it wasn't just that. Art wanted to please him, wanted to do anything possible to give Leo the same bliss he just experienced. He didn't really care what that took, and that overwhelmed everything else, even his lingering hetero doubts.

Maybe Leo could feel the direction of Art's thoughts as he stroked his hard dick. He threaded his fingers through Art's hair and yanked his head back, his big hand cradling Art's head. "You don't have to do anything, Art. Just being with you like this is more than enough for me."

"What makes you think I don't want to do more?"

"Nothing...but this is all very new to you. I guess I don't want to push you too far..." He turned his head away and muttered, "Or right out the door."

Art cupped Leo's cheek and prompted him back to meet his eyes. They were close enough to kiss, but Art just kept studying his face his friend's familiar, open face. He'd always been an open book, but now Art could read every word on his soul. This was more serious than just sex.

"You're not pushing me to do anything. I started this, remember? And I'm continuing it because I like it a lot, definitely more than I ever thought I would. And I like you a lot. Got that?"

Leo nodded. "Yeah, I do."

"Good. Now, no more interrupting me. I've got a lot of time to make up for."

"You don't..."

"Shh." He pressed a hard kiss to Leo's mouth, his bruised lips tingling at the pressure. He wrapped his fingers around Leo's cock with new firmness and pumped his wrist, adding a twist and a flourish every time he reached the swollen head. Leo gasped every single time, his cock jerking, his body melting into Art's arms.

Leo couldn't believe this was happening to him, especially since he'd been on a run of bad luck lately. While Art had been in The Zone, riding every bull with apparent ease, Leo had been struggling. Art acted like nothing strange was going on, but Leo was barely holding on to his place in the rankings, and if he didn't get a few good rides soon, he might slip to the bottom. That was why he brought up the possibility of retiring. He'd rather quit than be kicked off the professional circuit because he lost his ranking. Especially since there was only one distraction in his life, and he couldn't stand the thought of Art watching his fall from grace, not when Art was the very person distracting his thoughts from everything that once mattered to him.

He couldn't really understand why or how it happened. Art was objectively amazing, but so were most of the men Leo knew in the PBR. They were the best of the best, all of them exceptional in more ways than one. You didn't get this far without a tough spirit and a sharp mind, and those were qualities that Leo always respected and gravitated toward. But none of them were like Art. Nobody was like Art except Art, and Leo's obsession was a slow, gradual thing. A series of thoughts and feelings that built into an avalanche until Leo woke up one morning and realized that he hadn't thought about anybody but Art in a long time, maybe months.

From then on, it was impossible to deny or ignore his feelings. They were always there, pressing on his heart, because Art was always there, pressing on his life. He knew Art was straight and a big fan of, and a hit with, the ladies, so he never dared consider his chances. He never opened himself up to this possibility because for once in his life, he was a coward, afraid of the danger, afraid of the pain. He'd climb onto the back of a bull, a horse, or anything else that could flip him and kill him in an instant, but climbing on top of Art? That seemed like a tragedy too intense for him to survive.

And yet, here he was with Art. There they were together. He wasn't kidding when he told Art he didn't have to do anything. Getting to taste Art, getting to kiss him and pleasure him and feel the weight of his cock in his mouth, was already more than anything he could have ever hoped for. If it was all he ever got in his life, then it would be enough. But it wasn't all he was going to get. Not even close because Art had that look on his face and that certain shine in his eye. Leo knew it because he knew Art. He always looked a little like a mad man before throwing himself into a challenge. Honestly, it was one of the things he loved so much about his friend.

Art dropped to his knees, putting his mouth level with Leo's twitching head. He can already feel the flood of warmth at the base of his spine, and he knew he would not be able to hold off the explosion for long. He'd spent way too many nights with nothing but his own hand, and that was a very, very poor substitute for the person he wanted, for the mouth he longed to feel. And now that mouth was only an inch from his straining cock, so close that Leo could feel the heat coming off his lips. At first, he didn't do anything but study and examine. Leo was too busy studying Art's perfect face to be impatient, though. It wasn't often that he got to stare at Art, openly admiring the surprising beauty of his face. He was the sort who would never be called classically handsome, but there was a certain...poetry to his features. Leo would never, ever say that out loud, but it was the only way he could describe Art's face to himself. His lips were a full, pillowy pink, far too soft, and even feminine for the otherwise hard angles of his face. His nose was just a little too big (but it did indicate the rather spectacular length of his cock), and his ears jutted out too much. But his long, blond lashes framed the bluest eyes Leo had ever seen and his hair was golden and soft.

Art's tongue darted forward, the pink tip dancing over Leo's tender skin. It would have tickled if every tiny caress wasn't accompanied by a shockingly painful jolt to his groin. Leo moaned and leaned back, putting his hands flat on the table to support his weight. Art kept up the unknowing torture, his tongue wiggling and flicking over Leo's far-too-tight skin. He felt like he was going to crack right open, and when Art finally wiggled his tongue over his slit, fresh pre-cum oozed from him, slicking Art's pretty lips.

"Art...I need to feel more of your mouth...you're killing me here."

Art looked up with a boyish grin that Leo hadn't seen in months of watching Art's every expression. "Sorry. I kind of got all distracted there. Is this better?"

He parted his lips and sucked Leo into his mouth, his tongue wrapping around the tip as he hollowed his cheeks. He didn't stop at the crown though, his mouth sinking lower and lower until Leo could feel Art's soft palate. He stopped there, pulled back slightly, letting his tongue do most of the work as he held Leo there. It felt amazing but it wasn't going to be enough. He wanted to fuck Art's mouth, take away everything else and there was still that sizzling, undeniable fact. He wanted to clutch Art by the ears and fuck his throat raw – make him hoarse for the rest of the week so that every time he spoke he would remember Leo's cock buried in his throat, sawing in and out of the tender flesh.

But he was going to let Art take his time. He was going to let Art be the leader. He was going to let Art move at his own speed and on his own impulse and he'd be patient and...

"Leo?"

He whimpered out a "What?" already missing the heat of Art's mouth. His balls were tight and aching, and he was afraid that he'd snap at any second.

"Do you want to fuck me?"

What kind of question was that? "Let me fuck your throat."

"My gag reflex..."

"Don't worry about it. Just ride it out. Breathe through your nose. Trust me."

Art nodded. "Okay."

Leo took a deep breath and held Art's head between his palms, pressing on his ears. Art looked up with expecting, trusting eyes, and Leo felt another moment of doubt. What if he unleashed himself and Art realized he really, really didn't want that? What if they were both fooling themselves? It is a real possibility, but Leo couldn't muster more than a fleeting concern, because Art's mouth was right there and open and welcoming and he was going to get himself off at least once before everything went to hell.

Leo thrust his hips forward, driving his head all the way to the back of Art's throat. He did gag, as expected, but Leo held his head in place, using his superior strength to keep him still. He pushed harder and deeper, and Art gagged louder.

"Breathe through your nose," Leo reminded him, not relinquishing the ground he gained. For a terrible moment, it seemed like Art was going to fight him, do whatever necessary to get away from the fearful pressure at the back of his throat. Leo wouldn't let it come to that and wouldn't hold him if he really made a move to escape, but then something flickered across Art's face, and Leo knew he wasn't going to run. It was determination, an answer to a challenge. It was an automatic response, an integral part of him. The reason he was the best at everything.

Art finally took Leo's advice and inhaled deeply through his nose. He exhaled slowly and did it again, the alien pressure on the back of his throat nearly driving him to distraction. He wanted to cough it away and wanted to yank his mouth off before the sensation actually made him puke. But he trusted Leo and he knew he could do this. With another deep breath, he concentrated on relaxing his throat and sinking down to bury his nose in the soft red hair (Leo had the softest body hair Art ever felt on anybody, man or woman).

He started to move his head, sliding his mouth back and forth, though only a few inches at a time, leaving most of Leo buried between his lips. He kept his eyes open, looking up to get the full impact of Leo's reaction. The sounds coming out of his mouth are amazing, and his cock became fully erect again, each moan and whimper hitting him directly in the groin. Leo's eyes were open, too, and he never looked away from Art. It was hard not to feel a little self-conscious, but there was a look of such...awe...on his face that the showman in Art couldn't help but preen. He did love to have an audience, after all, and he'd never had one as adoring as his friend.

"Art...can I?"

Art nodded, mentally and physically bracing himself, but he couldn't prepare himself for Leo's sudden transformation. Suddenly, he wasn't the sweet good-natured man Art knew, but the hard athlete, the man who could stare down a bull. His body wasn't just tall and lanky, but strong and well-muscled, and his hands were coarse and rough and knew exactly how to guide the creature at his mercy. Art saw the transformation on his face, felt it in the pressure of his hands, and finally had no choice but to submit to it as Leo began to piston his hips.

He fucked Art's face with strokes that were almost brutal, each thrust slamming his crown down the curve of Art's throat. Every time he pushed forward, he blocked Art's air and then he yanked back with and slammed down so swiftly that Art couldn't even still a breath. He clutched at Leo's hips, doing his best to hold on while fresh heat gathered in his groin. He'd never been treated like this by anybody, never been used or fucked, and he never expected to like it as much as he did. It all felt good, even the bruising thrusts into his throat. He grunted and moaned every time Leo rocked his hips, every time his balls slapped against Art's chin, and every time Leo blocked a breath and pulled his hair and squeezed his ears.

"Art...I'm going to shoot..."

He felt Leo's cock twitch in his throat and felt his balls pull up and then the explosion of liquid heat, but Leo was so deep that Art couldn't taste him. He swallowed reflexively, coaxing the last of Leo's cum down his throat, doing it again and again until Leo finally pulled from his throat.

"Are you okay?" Leo asked before he even caught his breath.

Art nodded. "Thirsty."

"I'll get you a beer." He yanked Art to his feet, fisted his hair, and claimed his mouth in a hot, slick kiss. Art wrapped his arms around Leo and kissed him back with equal intensity, his cock jutting between them, sliding over Leo's naked thigh. "Thank you. That was...thank you."

"How 'bout that beer, huh?"

"Sure! And anything else you want."

"Anything?"

"Name it and it's yours."

Art smiled, accepting the cold bottle of beer and downing the whole thing in four long swallows. He could think of a few things he wanted from Leo, especially since the night was young and they didn't have to ride the next day.

5 A RARE BATH

Cas and his partner Danny spend long weeks on the trail and don't always have the money for a decent room or a bath when they do ride into town. But for once, they're practically rich, and Cas can't get himself a bathtub fast enough. Danny has been waiting for a bath for a long time too - only he knows something Cas doesn't know. Bath time is the perfect time to make his long delayed move and have it all.

With the money they made running a message into town, they had five silver dollars and three gold pieces between them. A veritable fortune that Danny immediately wanted to spend on grub and whiskey. Cas had a more responsible inclination and wisely hid the majority of it away, sacrificing a single dollar for Danny's appetites and another dollar for a room the two of them could share. It had been months since either of them had seen an actual bed, not to mention a bathtub. All Danny could talk about was stuffing his face, but Cas barely noticed. He had a one-track mind, and that meant getting into a hot bath as soon as humanly possible. It was included in the cost of the room, and two colored boys fetched the heated water from the kitchen and made four total trips to fill the tub.

Cas promised he'd join Danny later, and Danny promised he'd take a bath sooner or later, and they parted company, both focused on seeing to basic needs. Cas lost no time in stripping the filthy clothes from his body, happily shedding three weeks' worth of dust and mud and sweat. He'd use the bath water later to wash out his clothes, but in the meantime he tossed them on the back of the chair and worked on prying his boots off. His long underwear followed, and he took a moment to enjoy his blessed nudity - not even realizing he was standing right in front of the window and everybody on the main thoroughfare below got more than a glimpse of his toned chest, flat stomach, rippling back, and perfect ass. Even Danny caught a glimpse, and though it wasn't anything he hadn't already seen before, his eyes widened slightly and his heart might have tripped over itself.

The first touch of hot water to his wiggling toes was exquisite and scalding, and Cas wanted to cry tears of pure happiness. When he agreed to follow Danny west to seek their fortunes, it had never occurred to him that he would be leaving all of civilization behind. He sank into the water with a grateful sigh, folding his legs beneath him as he immersed himself in the high-sided tub. Bubbles coated the surface, and he added more soap, happily working up a good layer of suds. Relaxed for the moment, he dropped his head against the edge and closed his eyes, letting the tension, not to mention the aches and pains of living on the trail, drain from his body.

He lost track of time, hardly even noticing as the water cooled around him. It was still warmer than the streams and rivers made of spring's thaw - nothing but bitter cold water from the tops of the most bitter cold mountain peaks. However long he drifted there, it was enough time for Danny to eat, drink half a bottle of whiskey, and stomp back up to the room to disturb Cas's peace.

"You gave everybody quite the show."

"What are you talking about?"

Danny nodded at the window Cas had failed to notice before. "That's what I'm talking about. You just waved your willie in front of everybody."

Cas reddened. "I didn't...wave my willie...as you so eloquently put it. I may have briefly stood in front of the window..."

"Uh, no. There was nothing brief about it. I think you scandalized half the women in town."

Now there was no resisting the intense blush across his face and chest. He'd been so absorbed with thoughts of bathing that it really wouldn't surprise him if he lingered in front of the window for an extended amount of time. He didn't have anything to say in defense of himself, so he reached for the soap and rubbed it vigorously between his palms.

"I really thought you'd be done by now. What have you been doing up here?" Danny looked pointedly at the patch of water and suds directly above Cas's crotch. "Making sure your willie is good and clean?"

"I must have fallen asleep," Cas muttered, his embarrassment now complete. He wished Danny would just go away. He was almost willing to hand over another one of their precious silver dollars to encourage Danny to be on his way. But they couldn't really afford that, and he had no reason to be so humiliated. He didn't actually do anything wrong. That was an important point to remember.

"Must have. Well, I was counting on you being done by the time I got back," Danny said, taking his vest off and unstrapping his holster. His belt followed, and he was halfway to removing his boots before Cas realized what he meant to do.

"You mean you intend to bathe now?"

"That was my plan."

"I'll be done in just a few minutes. You're right; it isn't fair of me to hog the tub..." Though the water was still so delightfully warm and the suds were still so smooth.

"Don't rush. There's plenty of room for two people in that tub."

"What?" Cas barely fit comfortably. He wasn't so sure that Danny could wedge himself in, and even if he could...well wouldn't that make them all a bit uncomfortably close? "No, I don't think that'll work at all."

"Don't be so fussy. I know for a fact that it'll work. I've done it before."

"You've bathed with another man before?" Cas asked, shocked.

"What? No, not another man. I mean, I've done it plenty of time with whores."

"Then I don't really see how you think it'll work with me." Cas didn't know why he was still talking about it. He put his hands on the side and lifted himself to his feet, but Danny's large palm on his shoulder stopped him from standing completely. He pushed Cas back to his seated position, forcing him to remain mostly submerged in the water.

"Just sit tight." Danny smiled at him - the smile that meant he was done talking about the issue - and returned to undressing. He peeled his filthy shirt off, and stepped out of his pants, then made short work of his long underwear. By the time that disappeared, Cas couldn't even pretend to be focused on anything else. Danny was, without a doubt, the most beautiful person Cas had ever known. He knew he wasn't supposed to look at his friend that way, that it was wrong to want to touch or kiss another man. But none of the girls he'd ever laid with excited his senses the way Danny did.

And that was ultimately why they couldn't share a tub. Cas' cock was already stirring with interest, and if Danny climbed into the tub, forced their legs and their groins to touch, put his beautiful chest and back within touching distance, his small amount of interest would definitely expand. There would be no hiding his response, and what would Danny think of him then? He had no other friends west of the Mississippi, and no money to get himself back home. If Danny turned away from him in disgust, sent him packing or just flat out abandoned him there, what would he do? Where would he turn? The risk was simply too great, and this time he didn't give Danny a chance to stop him.

"Hey. Where are you going?"

"I'm clean," Cas said stiffly. "And you deserve to enjoy the tub to its fullest."

Danny's mouth thinned into a line of displeasure, and Cas didn't understand why this had to be a fight. He had his turn, now Danny could have his turn, and none of them would be left to deal with an awkward and potentially painful situation. But Danny wasn't going to let anything be that easy, and he took Cas' arm, holding him still as he stepped over the side of the tub. They stood toe to toe, groin to groin, and no, this wasn't good. His mind knew the proper response, but his body didn't care.

"You sure don't make this easy for a guy, do you?"

"Make what easy?" Cas asked dumbly.

"I've been...entertaining certain thoughts. And I thought, perhaps, you've been entertaining the same ones. So, I thought, maybe we ought to do less thinking and more acting. You know?"

Cas could only stare silently. Danny couldn't truly be implying what Cas thought he was. Perhaps it was some sort of trick. Why his best friend would play such a cruel trick, Cas didn't know, but it was the only explanation that made sense.

"No? Yes? Cas, you gotta give me something here, or I'm going to start feeling very stupid."

"I..." What was he supposed to say?

Danny was never good with his words. Actions were always his strong suit. He moved quickly, reaching out to cup Cas's member. He massaged the flesh, digging the heel of his hand into the tender organ until it started to grow and harden. Danny smiled, wrapping his fingers around the length to stroke Cas into his full erection.

"Do you like that? Hmm?"

"Yes," Cas whispered weakly, still wary of a trap.

"Do you want me to stop?"

"No."

"Then get back in the tub."

Cas sank down into the water without another word, gripping the sides of the tub as he stared up at Danny's beautiful, imposing body. His cock was as hard as Cas's, jutting from between his thighs. The sight of his hard member did strange thing to Cas's midsection. Everything inside of him seemed to liquefy and shift places. Danny slowly lowered himself to his knees, straddling Cas's legs, shifting so their dicks slid together. He gripped both shafts in one fist, stroking up and down, letting their slippery skin slide back and forth. It felt heavenly, and Cas exhaled in stunned pleasure, unsure if he was even allowed to experience something so amazing. Surely, this was wrong, and surely it must stop.

But Danny was never one to concern himself with questions of right and wrong. He was a simple creature, driven by the most basic wants and needs. Ultimately, if it felt good, if it numbed the pain, if it provided even an ounce of satisfaction, then Danny was a fan. And this definitely felt good. Sparks flowed under his skin, igniting from every point of contact between them. A new slickness spread across his skin, and he realized it was fresh arousal. He was leaking the clear fluid rather freely; another telltale sign of just how much Danny affected him. But Danny either didn't notice or didn't care, his fingers flying up and down their members.

"Cas...do you want to kiss me?"

Cas swallowed hard and nodded, but didn't make any move to fulfill his desires.

Danny smiled his crooked smile. "Then do it. You may not get another chance like this one."

Cas recognized the wisdom in that suggestion. Especially since he had no idea what led to this particular chance presenting itself. If he didn't claim Danny's full, pink lips he would spend the rest of his life wondering just what he was missing out on. Of course, it might be worse to know. When he kept himself awake deep into the night, torturing himself with thoughts of everything he couldn't have, did he really want to add the memory of Danny's lips to that list? Oh, what the hell was he thinking? Of course it was better to have the memory of something real over the fantasy of something coveted.

He cupped the back of Danny's head and slammed their mouths together, pouring himself into the forceful kiss. If this was his one shot, he was going to do his best to make it count. His lips were chapped and he tasted of the cheap moonshine he bought downstairs, but Cas caught the hint of something more beneath that. Eager to taste Danny, Cas pushed his tongue between his full lips, demanding his entrance. Danny parted his lips without hesitation, welcoming Cas inside, and he was relieved they were seated, because otherwise his knees would have turned to water and he would have tumbled to the ground.

Cas lost himself in the kiss, far too caught up in it to worry about anything else. Danny continued to stroke them, his fist sending drops of water flying around them on every downward stroke. The firmness of Danny's palm, the roughness of his fingers, the heat of his flesh, the sheer fact he was touching Cas at all, unlocked new realms of pleasure for Cas. Just a few minutes before Danny walked into the room, Cas had been convinced that nothing could ever feel as good as a quiet soak in the tub. Now he was climbing to new heights of pleasure, and there could still be so much more between them. He had no way of anticipating what Danny might do, which direction he'd steer the two of them.

"I want to feel you inside of me," Danny said against his mouth.

Cas reeled back, too stunned to make a sound of agreement or protest. Surely, Danny didn't mean that? Perhaps this was some sort of vivid fever dream, or a drug-induced hallucination. Somebody could have laced his food with enough opiates to make him see pink elephants. Not entirely likely, true, but was it anymore unlikely than...this?

"You don't have to," Danny said in a rush. "I'll understand if you don't want to. Not everybody does...or would..."

Cas finally found his voice. "Have you done this before?"

Danny nodded. "I've tried a few times. I liked it. But like I said, if you don't want to..."

"I want to," Cas said, surprising both of them.

"You sure?"

"I'm sure."

Danny smiled and reached for a bottle of hair oil and coaxed Cas from his seated position, lifting his dick above the water. Danny quickly slicked Cas's shaft, spreading the oil from his base to his tip, squeezing the heated flesh until Cas moaned. He reached behind him, spreading the slick on his fingers to his waiting ass. Cas swallowed again as he watched Danny carefully finger himself. He couldn't see Danny's finger disappearing into his ass, but he could see the moment when concentration and pain gave way to pleasure. His eyes fluttered shut and his face went lax, his full lips parting and his head dropping back. He was beautiful, and if Cas had any lingering fears or reservations, they were gone in that moment. Maybe this was wrong and God sent sodomites to the darkest pits of Hell, but Cas couldn't help but feel that this was between himself and Danny, and God wasn't really welcome to interfere or have any part in it.

"Won't it hurt?" Cas asked, as Danny positioned himself, his pucker resting against Cas's blunt tip.

"Yeah, but that's kind of why I like it. So don't worry about hurting me, okay?"

"I don't know what to do," Cas admitted.

"Sure you do. You've gotten your dick wet before, haven't you? Just slide it home and we're golden."

That was easier said than done. Despite the oil on his length and Danny's ass, he couldn't just slide it home. He was much thicker than Danny's opening, and Danny was still very, very tight. Danny's face scrunched up and twisted as Cas pushed past the opening, barely gaining an inch. He almost wanted to stop there - well, that wasn't quite true. Once he felt that tight heat around his crown, he wanted more. But he didn't want to see the discomfort on Danny's face, didn't want to carry the guilt of hurting his friend.

"Do it," Danny spit out between clenched teeth.

"What?" Cas asked helplessly.

"Take me. Like you want to." Danny gripped Cas' shoulders and wiggled his hips. "Come on. I chose you for a reason, Cas. Don't disappoint me."

Cas only ever wanted one thing from Danny - his love. And if he couldn't have that, then he'd settle for the other man's affection and approval. Now it seemed like all three were on the line, hanging in the balance of Cas' performance. He felt a certain calmness fall over him, and he gripped Danny by the hips, holding him in place while he drove his own hips up and forward, pushing past all the resistance of Danny's body to fill him, claim him.

"Oh that's IT. Yes...yes...Cas! Oh fuck me, fuck me, fuck me. Please fuck me."

That was the first time Cas ever heard Danny say please, and it did something weird and wonderful to him. He felt the last of his doubts and insecurities fall away, and there was nothing stopping him from giving Danny the pounding he wanted - the one he deserved. He didn't notice the water splashing noisily over the side of the tub, or the way the soap and the sponges flew to the ground from the force of their coupling. Cas forgot about being exhausted, sore, and a thousand miles from home. He forgot about his earlier embarrassment. Nothing mattered except the pressure of Danny constricting around his dick each time he slammed down to meet one of Cas' powerful thrusts.

Cas knew one thing for sure - none of the girls he'd paid for ever made him feel like this. He kissed Danny with plain hunger, explored his body with reckless abandon, touched every scar and every wound and every mark he didn't know the origin of. He followed the line of his spine, the jut of his hips, and the perfect map of his torso. He kissed what he could reach with his mouth, caressed what he couldn't, and never lost sight of the real prize. Danny's full force and strength flexing around his body, gripping and pumping his dick.

He wasn't going to last long in Danny's ass, as tight as it was. He tried to say as much, but when he realized his warning wasn't fast enough, it turned into a strangled apology as he shot his seed deep into Danny's bowels. Danny kept rocking down on his cock, not really giving him a chance to soften, while he stroked himself in rhythm with the fucking. Cas fisted Danny's hair and their lips clashed once again, Cas using his teeth and tongue to invade and overwhelm his mouth. His grunt vibrated over Cas' lips, the only warning before his hot load splattered across Cas' chest and dripped into the cooling water.

Danny moaned and dropped his brow to Cas' shoulder, panting for breath and trembling while the aftershocks of his pleasure rolled through him. Cas put an arm around him, holding him even closer, greedily taking every second of contact he could get.

"Cas?"

"Hmm?"

"This doesn't have to be a one-time thing. I mean, think about it. You don't have to say anything now. But...you should know that."

Cas smiled to himself. He'd already done all the thinking he needed to do. And this definitely wasn't going to be a one-time thing.

6 A RARE BED

This wasn't the first time Cas and Danny slept side by side. It wasn't even the first time they shared a bed. But it was the first time they shared a bed after having sex, and Cas wasn't sure exactly what was now expected of him.

Could he reach across the strip of bed separating them and rest his hand on Danny's chest? Could he rest his head on his shoulder? Could he wake up in the middle of the night and curl up close to the other man's heat?

Danny always kept his distance from the world, didn't like it when other people touched him, and until that afternoon in the tub, never gave any indication that he thought about touching other people.

Fucking Danny in the tub had been one

of the most intensely pleasurable and satisfying experiences of Cas's life. It wasn't the first time he had sex, but it was the first time he had sex with a partner he really, really wanted. The first time that sex could count as a "first time" rather than just a one-off before he left town again. Meaningful relationships were few and far between in Cas's world. In fact, Danny counted as his only real friend-- and for most of their acquaintanceship, Danny had been nothing more but a business partner. Now he didn't really know what Danny was to him, what he was to Danny, and what was expected from him.

He needed to sleep. He knew he should get some shut eye, let his exhausted body and tired brain rest before puzzling over this question. He wouldn't get any real, true answers, and in his state, he was liable to make some mistake of logic, have some error in his thoughts. Danny slept beside him, his chest rising and falling in a known rhythm, the sounds of his sleep as familiar to Cas as his own name. He was used to taking first watch, used to sitting up beside a sleeping Danny, watching a fire and listening to the darkness for any sounds of danger. But that wasn't necessary here. They were never exactly safe, but it was far safer behind a locked door in the middle of civilization--or at least what passed for civilization out here on the frontier. There were no Indians, no wild animals, and no danger lurking in the shadows.

This meant he could focus all of his attention on Danny's sleeping form, and he was doing exactly that. He mostly stared at the ceiling and out the window--or at least he tried to. But his attention kept going back to Danny, his eyes slipping to his relaxed face, to the shade of his eyelashes and the shape of his mouth. It seemed like it might be okay to touch him--well when he was awake. Touching Danny while he slept was never a good plan. He lashed out first and asked questions later. Cas learned that one the hard way. But he wasn't opposed to Cas in general. In fact, what had he said? He chose Cas. He wanted Cas more than anybody else. He trusted Cas more than anybody else, and that was the most unbelievable and wonderful part of all.

His thoughts were still churning when his body finally gave up and forced his eyes closed. His mind kept chugging right along, his thoughts turning to dreams--graphic, sweaty, passionate dreams. He didn't just relive their coupling in the tub, but worked through all kinds of scenarios--some he considered before--and some were completely new. When he woke up, he was hard as a rock, covered in sweat, and pinned to the mattress by Danny's amused gaze.

"I think I know what you were dreaming," he teased gently.

"I..." Cas wasn't even sure what to say. "Was I talking in my sleep?"

"You were doing far more than that. Moaning and panting and...well, let's just say that I was quite impressed with my dream self's skill."

Cas blushed a deep red. He'd hoped at the very least that he wouldn't betray his own secrets, but apparently that was too much to hope for. "Um...sorry."

"Why are you apologizing?"

"I must have waked you."

His lips quirked. "You know, hearing you panting my name is just about the most pleasant way anybody's ever woke me. Usually it's just a kick to the ribs or a bucketful of cold water. On one memorable occasion, it was a bullet."

Cas frowned. "Is that where the scar in your leg came from?"

"Yep."

"I thought you said you got it in Arizona?"

"I was in Arizona. The only thing I lied about was what I was doing at the time. Rustling cattle is much better than oversleeping my rendezvous. Don't you think?"

"Yeah, that does make a better story."

Danny was supporting his head on the palm of his hand, his elbow propped up on the pillow. The sheet was pushed down to his hips, and it only barely covered his groin. It felt like Cas had never, ever seen him like this before. He searched the images in his memory, but he was sure that this was a completely new look, a completely new pose to go along with their completely new situation. His questions from the night before came flooding back, but this time he didn't want to mull over those, he wanted to act. He wanted to find his answers. So he moved, reaching over the few inches between them to slide his fingers over the hair on Danny's chest. Danny glanced down, following his finger with his eyes but not making any move to stop or reciprocate. He simply watched, waiting to see what Cas was going to do.

He trailed his fingertips from Danny's throat to his waist, and then skimmed his palm back up over his ribs. Muscles twitched and jumped beneath his touch, and he found the indents and raised lines of scars everywhere he touched. Danny's life before they fell in together had been violent and brutal. Even as a child, he'd had a rough time of it. Some of the scars Cas felt and saw had to be almost as old as the man himself. How many times had he thought about doing this very thing? Every time he caught a glimpse of Danny without his shirt, his fingers itched to touch. It was automatic. It was nature and lust. What could he do about it except give in? That was never really an option before, but it was now.

Cas went up his neck and followed the line of his stubbly jaw to his chin. He'd stopped at the barber the day before for a shave, and now his jaw had a rough texture that made Cas ache. He wanted to feel that texture on his lips, but pure shyness stopped him from leaning forward to skim his lips over his skin. Instead, he used the back of his fingers, sliding back and forth and then down to his square jaw. There was a dimple right in the middle. One Cas never noticed before because of Danny's beard. It made him look oddly boyish, growing deeper when he smiled. Cas brushed his thumb over the small indent, too captivated to notice that Danny was moving, leaning closer and closer, until they were close enough to share breath.

"Good morning," Danny breathed before touching their lips together. The kiss was as tentative as Cas felt, as though Danny secretly harbored the same doubts and questions. The thought was remarkable, really. Danny wasn't the sort of man who harbored doubts, and if he had questions, he made them known--though he rarely had questions. He usually knew everything, understood everything, and had a plan for every contingency. He'd survived a long time out on the frontier, dodging Indians and his own fellow bandits and cutthroats. He once told Cas "he who hesitates is lost" and Cas had agreed with that logic, though it had done very little to impact Cas's naturally cautious nature. The thought that maybe Danny was as confused as him buoyed his confidence, and he held the back of Danny's head, pulling him closer, deepening the kiss with a sweep of his tongue.

Danny made a soft sound in his throat and opened to the caress, welcoming Cas's tongue. Somehow, they were moving, shifting together, so that Danny was flat on his back and Cas was over him, his body half covering Danny's. They were both naked and their skin slid together like fine silk, slippery and silent. Cas had never considered himself a big kisser, but he couldn't get enough of the way Danny's mouth moved beneath his. He couldn't get enough of the tiny noises he made, the small groans and grunts of encouragement. His prick was harder than ever, and he found himself shifting his hips, grinding his member against Danny's thigh. He dragged his hand down Danny's body until his palm found his stiff cock. He closed his fingers around it and squeezed hard. Danny gasped, his hips shooting up, his hands suddenly tight where he held Cas against him.

Cas moved to position himself directly over Danny's body, lowering himself so their chests touched, his knees straddling Danny's hips. He reached between their bodies and wrapped his hand around both shafts, rubbing them together. He could feel Danny's pulse vibrating through his own flesh, and his heart jolted, as if it watched to catch up to Danny's pace. Their mouths remained sealed together, though Danny's kiss was shifting, becoming more brutal and demanding. The sort of kiss Cas would expect from a man like Danny.

His hips came down and Danny's shifted up again, their bodies rocking together while Cas pumped his wrist, stroking them both. It felt fucking amazing, and he knew Danny would say the same. They were both leaking copious amounts of liquid, and it touched slick and cool on his knuckles and his palm and spread over his shaft. He pulled away from the kiss, pausing long enough to spit into the palm of his hand to help encourage the wet feel. He wanted to be inside Danny again and he had the feeling that Danny agreed with that sentiment.

Once their dicks were both slick from tip to base, Cas released them and slipped his hand lower, deeper between Danny's legs, nudging his heavy sac out of the way so he could reach his asshole. He teased the pucker, trying to lube up the tight muscle before slipping one finger inside. He knew Danny could take that easily, so he didn't hesitate to slide all the way to his knuckle. Danny moaned between gritted teeth, legs falling open even wider, giving Cas as much access as possible. Was he ready for another round? Or was he still sore from the night before? He certainly seemed ready, but Cas didn't want to cause him any real pain or distress. Especially since they were riding out of town soon and Cas couldn't imagine a sore ass was a great thing to have on the back of a horse.

"I want you, Cas. I want you to fuck me."

"Are you sure?"

"How many different ways do I have to show you? How many different times do I have to tell you?"

"I just don't want to hurt you."

"You won't," he murmured, hooking his legs around Cas's waist, pulling him close. "So let's put that big prick of yours to good use, yeah?"

Cas nodded. Yeah, they should do that. Yeah, he definitely wanted that too. Yeah, he was going to do it even if he was worried about Danny's comfort, because his ass felt too fucking amazing. Only a fool would pass up on the opportunity, and Cas's mama didn't raise no fool. He pumped his wrist, stroking in and out of Danny a few times before adding a second finger. Danny's muscled walls stretched easily around the second digit, and he jerked his hips with what could only be called impatience. Cas smiled too himself because that was so, so Danny. Everything had to be on his own time and just the way he wanted it. Cas never minded accommodating his partner's control issues, but that would change soon enough. Soon, he would take the time to show Danny the virtue of patience, show him how good something could be with a little bit of waiting, a little build up. Show him how good it could be when you didn't insist on controlling every little thing.

"I'm ready, Cas." Danny choked out when the impatient roll of his hips failed to get him what he wanted.

"You sure?"

"Never been more sure of anything. And stop asking me that."

"Yes, sir." Cas pulled his fingers free and lined his cock up to Danny's ass. He was still wet with pre-cum, though he didn't think it was enough. Danny didn't seem to care. He tightened his legs around Cas and arched his hips up, lifting most of his back from the bed to meet Cas's dick. Cas gripped him by the waist, holding him with hard, inflexible fingers, and eased forward. Like the night before, it was difficult at first. Danny was so tight and there wasn't enough slick. He should have thought to grab oil this time, but now there wasn't any time to act. Danny wasn't going to release him. Wasn't going to be happy with anything less than a full, hard thrust.

Cas thrust as hard as he did the night before, using his full strength to penetrate the tight ring and bury himself up to his balls. Danny closed his fingers around the straining muscles in Cas's arms, bracing himself as he rose even higher. They both relaxed at the same time, Cas easing out about half way before tensing. They slammed their bodies together with echoing grunts, the force almost enough to make Cas's teeth rattle. Then another slow separation and an equally violent coming together again. They did it again and again until they were following a pattern, slow and hard, the perfect combination of restraint and power. Cas's head was swimming with pleasure almost immediately, and that only flowed downward, filling his entire body. The only thing that felt better than fucking Danny was watching him. His body was stretched out and taut, skin gleaming with sweat in the early morning light, his skin a deep brown compared to the muslin sheet. He admired Danny like he admired the finest horses--with pure respect and more than a little awe.

Cas had the ability and the control to keep the rhythm exactly as they established it, even when his heart started racing faster and faster and hips tried to get away from him. Even when Danny clenched down so hard around Cas's dick he didn't think he'd be able to move at all. And when Danny suddenly changed his own tempo, trying to urge Cas into an even faster, harder speed, Cas resisted as long as he could, but it was too hard. Too painful, even. Something inside of him snapped, a roar building and escaping from deep within his chest. Danny's flushed face split into a smile at the sound and then they were off to the races. Their new tempo was brutal, far too fast for anything like control. Far too fast to withstand for long. The headboard pounded relentlessly against the back wall, each thump echoed in their shared moans. They were loud. So loud the whole damned township probably heard them, but Cas didn't really care. He didn't care about anything except Danny's body moving beneath him and clenching around him.

"Oh fuck...fuck Cassy, fuck I'm close.

Oh I'm going to..." And then Danny's cock jerked, and his cum flew everywhere, landing in long strings on Cas's chest and splashing back to his own stomach. His walls clenched around Cas's dick again, but this time, he couldn't pretend it wasn't the most exquisite, amazing tightness, heat, perfection he ever felt. He thrust forward one more time, filling Danny completely before shooting his own load deep inside.

"Fuck," he sighed, collapsing into Danny's welcoming arms.

"Now that's what I call a great way to wake up."

"Mmmm," Cas agreed, nuzzling into the crook of Danny's neck where he still smelled like sleep. "Tired."

"Go to sleep then. We don't have anywhere to be."

"Thanks."

"No," Danny said from a growing distance. "Thank you."

7 ON THREE

Clint just wants to show his old friend a good time and maybe have a few laughs. So the strip club was a mistake. How was he supposed to know Steve would be so damned uncomfortable? Clint thinks their friendship has just turned stale in the five years since Steve moved from town, but Steve wants more than friendship. And now, he can finally tell Clint the truth.

It may have been five years since Clint saw his best friend, but he could still read Steve like an open book. Something was seriously troubling him. Nobody should look that sad in the middle of a tittie bar. He barely seemed aware of the fact that he was surrounded by mostly naked women, and when a few of the girls got too close, he shooed them away like he was batting at a fly. Clint was more than a little put out. He liked this bar, and he liked these girls, and he thought Steve would have a good time. Had his friend really changed that much in five years?

"You hungry? We can go pick up a burger. I know a place that's still open."

Steve shook his head. "I'm fine."

"Okay, fine. Do you just want to get out of here?"

"We should stay. You're having a good time."

No, he really wasn't. Maybe if Steve didn't look like he was watching kittens getting tortured. His long face was bringing down the whole joint. They had to get out of there, even if Steve insisted he was fine, or else he'd have the girls too depressed to dance in no time. He slapped a pile of ones on the table, downed the last of his beer, and stood. "Come on, let's go."

"We really don't have to..."

But Clint was already walking. He smiled at the girls, and a few of the familiar patrons, walking with calm strides while Steve hurried to catch up with him, keeping well out of the reach of the girls. Maybe he doesn't want to get cooties Clint thought as held the door open for his friend. The night air was much cooler and fresher without the smell of sweat and booze and desperation. Steve took a big, relieved breath, and they turned to where Clint had parked.

"You okay, man?"

"I'm fine. Why do you think I'm not?"

"Why didn't you just tell me you didn't want to go out drinking?"

"I did want a drink. I just...I guess I'm just tired. You know, a long day of traveling and I think I'm a bit jet-lagged."

"I can drive you back to your hotel."

"Thanks. I appreciate it."

Clint swallowed down his disappointment, locking it in his stomach. When he learned Steve was coming home after five years absence—four in college and one "traveling abroad"—he thought it would be like old times. Except this time all of their favorite things—tittie bars and booze chief among them—were legal and easily accessible. Steve seemed to have been on board with the plan, but now Clint could see he was just playing along because he was a nice guy. He probably didn't think he had anything left to say to Clint anymore, and he was probably right. What did they have in common? He had a BS in Chemical Engineering, and Clint barely finished his time at the air-conditioning repair annex. Steve has seen the world. Clint never made it further than Las Vegas for the Twenty-Four Hour Challenge.

Steve's hotel was closer to the airport

than to his hometown, and they made the forty-minute drive in silence. Clint could feel Steve's eyes on him, but he didn't turn his head, gave no sign of noticing at all. He looked different now, too. He used to be scrawny and skinny, the sort of boy who could eat five thousand calories in a day and not even move the scale a half inch. Now, he looked more like an MMA fighter. Still narrow, but definitely not scrawny. Did he know how to fight now, or did he just have the physique? It had been quite the challenge to stop himself from staring, redirecting his attention back to the girls every time he felt his gaze linger on his former best friend for too long. Honestly, that was the chief reason for choosing that particular establishment.

Clint pulled his car into the circular drop-off area at the door, leaving the engine idling. "Well, Steve, it was really great seeing you. We should definitely do this again sometime."

"Yeah, we should."

"How long will you be in town?"

"A few weeks. My new position doesn't open up until the first of July, so I'm just unwinding for a while."

What did he do to unwind? But Clint knew the answer to his own question—he read books. He always had a book in front of his face when they were kids. How did they ever become friends? Were things always this strained and he just never noticed it before?

"I'm sorry about tonight. Actually...there was something I wanted to tell you. I wanted to wait for the perfect time...but I guess there's no such thing as that."

"What is it?"

"I'm gay, Clint."

Clint pursed his lips. "You could have mentioned that before the brilliant idea to go to the tittie bar, buddy."

"You're not angry?"

"No, why would I be angry?"

"In high school you were...quite vocal about David Domingo. You remember him?"

"Yeah...yeah, I remember him." He even remembered what he said. Nothing he was proud of. Plenty of things he eventually apologized for, though David himself didn't appear to remember any of it. "I was a complete jerk, and I'm really sorry about that. But...he...he scared me."

"So you were literally homophobic?"

Clint laughed a little. "Yeah, I guess so."

"Why did he scare you?"

"Because I wanted what he had, I guess. I was confused. Everybody made it seem like it was one or the other, and my interests weren't just limited to girls."

"So you're bisexual?"

"Yeah."

Steve let that sink in for a moment.

"Why don't you walk me to my room." It wasn't a question. It wasn't really even an invitation. Steve was always a bit bossy.

"I don't know if..."

Steve cut off his protest with a kiss, their lips fitting well together. At first, Clint couldn't move. The pressure against his mouth was too strange. He couldn't believe it was even happening. Did he want it to happen? Hadn't he always wanted it to happen? Even when Steve weighed a hundred pounds soaking wet and seemed to have an allergic reaction to physical activity and sunshine, Clint had wanted to kiss him. Wasn't that why David Domingo really freaked him out? Because somewhere deep inside, he resented that David could have boyfriends and Clint couldn't even kiss the boy he loved.

Still loved. Because he was still Steve.

Clint parted his lips, surrendering to the kiss, welcoming Steve's tongue as it slipped into his mouth. He forgot that he was parked in front of a busy hotel, forgot about the years of conditioning and training trying to remind him that this was wrong. The pleasure was like a thick elixir traveling down his throat, spreading warmth through his chest. He tasted Steve's desire and even sensed the sharp edge of desperation. Like he was going to take all that he could get in whatever limited time they had.

Did Steve come back for him? No, Clint wasn't going to let himself think that way. He didn't want to build up his own hopes just so reality could knock them down in the morning. He wouldn't think about the future or possible motivations, only the moment they were in, only the caresses they were sharing.

"Come upstairs with me."

This time, Clint only nodded. He put the car in drive, swung around to the nearest parking spot, and then removed the keys with trembling fingers. This was happening, and he wasn't going to stop it, and he didn't think Steve would take back his invitation. His stomach rolled as they walked through the building, and his palms were hot and clammy. He kept trying to dry them off on the sides of his legs, but that was a temporary solution at best. Steve seemed calm, though, crossing the lobby to the elevator, smiling at the girl behind the reception desk. He punched the button labeled six, and the doors whooshed close behind them. Past the point of no return, Clint thought.

Steve's room was at the end of a long corridor, and Clint fell a step behind to watch the way his tight ass moved beneath his pants. It was...nice. Okay, it was more than nice. It was really fucking magnificent, and Clint was not going to be able to keep his hands or mouth off his round-as-a-peach bottom. He was still staring when Steve slid his key card into the lock, and he didn't glance away in time.

"Like my ass?"

"It's not bad."

Steve smiled for the first time that night, and Clint cursed himself for his stupidity. He'd wasted a whole night for no good reason, but at least now they had a chance to rectify that.

Clint kicked the door shut behind him and advanced on Steve, backing him up to the wall, cornering him there and moving in for the kiss. He teased Steve for a moment, then skimmed his lips across his strong jaw, detecting the slightly rough texture of his fresh, blond stubble. His nostrils flared, mentally cataloguing the scent of him, filing it away with the feel of him, and the way he made Clint's pulse race like he was a teenage virgin. They should have been virgins together, should have taken each other's cherries, but maybe it was better this way. At least now, neither one of them would be inexperienced and scared. Steve turned his head slightly, catching Clint's mouth in a slow, searching kiss. Clint sighed, the room spinning around him as Steve's tongue dipped into his mouth with promising thoroughness.

He needed to feel Steve's skin. He tugged at the taller man's shirt, breaking away from the kiss just long enough to yank the shirt overhead. His own quickly followed, and when their mouths rejoined, their bare torsos touched, Clint's rough hair sliding against Steve's smooth skin. That wasn't enough, though. Clint needed to use his hands. He traced the defined curve of every muscle on his shoulders and down his back, delighted by how firm he was, how beautifully his skin flowed over thick muscle. He seemed bigger somehow, like he found a way to grow three or four inches taller while he was gone. But that was just an illusion, encouraged by the fact that he'd grown in every other way.

His cock formed a hard bulge in his pants, and Steve's bulge pressed against his hip. Clint pulled his pants open, moaning as Steve returned the favor with his long fingers. He shoved those fingers into Clint's boxers and pulled his cock out, the tips gliding over his head before he closed his fist around the throbbing shaft.

"Just like I remembered," Steve murmured so softly that Clint wasn't sure he was supposed to hear it. He pulled back slightly to meet Clint's eyes. "I want you to fuck me. I've wanted it...god for about as long as I knew what sex was."

"That's...an awfully long time."

"You're telling me. It feels more like an eternity."

"Condom?"

"I have some and lube." He stepped away from the wall and pulled Clint with him, moving towards the room's plus king-sized mattress. There was plenty of room for the two of them to get a little athletic. Hell, there was plenty of room for two other people to get athletic right alongside them. Steve pulled a box of condoms and a small bottle of lube from the bag sitting on the foot then tossed it to the floor. He quickly kicked off his pants and then flung himself face down on the mattress with puppy-like eagerness. But Clint had to take a moment to simply stare, mouth slightly agape, eyes wide, as the feast now before him.

Fuck, he was beautiful. Fuck, fuck, when did that happen? Fuck.

Clint's fingers trembled slightly as he tore at the foil and unrolled the condom. He crawled onto the bed with the lube in hand and took Steve by the hips, guiding them up so his ass popped out. Steve's body was lanky and chiseled, his cock full and long, hanging between his legs. They would have to switch at some point, because Clint wanted Steve's dick as much as he wanted his ass. He pulled his fleshy cheeks apart and poured lube down the crack, spreading it over and in and out of his clenched pucker. When he slipped his finger inside, Steve rose to meet him, moaning at the first contact and not stopping for one second after that. Clint grinned. Oh, he was that kind of bottom was he?

"Do you need to be stretched?"

"No...no...just fuck me, Clint. I'm ready, I promise."

So was Clint. His cock was hard enough to hammer nails with, and the rolling in his stomach had turned to a hard clench in his lower abdomen. His groin ached, the tip of his dick straining for the heaven promised between his best friend's legs. He pressed his head to the slick ring, one hand holding Steve's hip, the other gliding up and down his back. That was the hand he used to guide Steve, gently urging him back until his mushroom head disappeared inside Steve's channel. He pushed his hips forward then, automatically seeking more of that impossibly tight, raging heat. Steve was going to set him on fire, making him burn from the inside out, starting with the blood roaring down from his head to fill his cock, making him dizzy and harder than ever before.

"Oh yes...oh yes...oh yes...oh good God Clint what the fuck...oh..."

Clint paused, alarmed. "Are you hurt?"

"No! Don't stop. Please give me that monster cock. Please fuck me."

"Yeah, no problem, buddy. No problem at all." He claimed the final inches, sliding forward to sheath himself fully. He had to catch his breath once he was seated there, but Steve had other minds, and instead of giving Clint the ten seconds of stillness he needed, he twitched and bucked, rocking forward and sliding back, and Clint thought that was it, he was going to fucking lose it. Both hands went to Steve's hips and he held him in place.

"God, give me a minute."

Steve moaned in protest, his head dropping down like it was too heavy to lift any longer. Clint watched the muscles ripple and move beneath his unmarred skin, fluttering with anticipation while he waited for Clint to break the stasis between them. Even if he concentrated on baseball stats and images of Steve's grandmother in her birthday suit, he wasn't going to be able to last for long. It was just too much to withstand. All of it, from the pressure of Steve's ass clamping down on him to the fact that he was with Steve at all.

Slow, slow, slow. Take it slow. One long, even breath at a time. He exhaled and pulled out, trying to free his cock from the crushing pressure that seemed to want to keep him trapped in place. He inhaled just as slowly, working his way back inside, his smooth skin sliding easily with the lube. Steve gripped him and nearly ruined everything. Clint moaned, his balls starting to pull tight.

"Fuck...fuck..." Clint panted.

"It's okay, man. I'm really close, too."

"You're not just saying that?"

"No, definitely not just saying it. Touch my cock."

He reached beneath Steve's body, the back of his hand brushing against his head and coming away slick with pre-come. He smeared it around with his fingers, making his palm slick before he fisted the length. He squeezed as hard as Steve's ass squeezed him—which was a slightly bad idea since it only encouraged Steve to stiffen, his muscles clenching even tighter.

"Let's move on three," Steve forced out. "And whatever happens, after that happens."

Clint knew exactly what was going to happen. A mess. "On three."

"One."

"Two."

"Three. Just fuck me Clint please."

Clint didn't think he would go much beyond the count of three himself, but the mental chains holding his hips in place snapped, and he didn't need any more encouragement. He unleashed himself, pounding into Steve's ass with hard, demanding thrusts, his fist moving with equal speed up and down Steve's shaft. He didn't cum right away, but the pleasure slamming through him was undeniable, overwhelming. He'd never ever felt anything as good as Steve's ass, and every clench and flutter was magnified by about a hundred times. Clint's body throbbed, his not-inadequate muscles flexing, fueling his powerful thrusts.

"Yes," Steve shouted. "Yes, oh yes, oh fuck Clint yes like that thank you thank you fuck yes."

"I can't..." Last much longer. But Steve's cock jerked, and suddenly his hand was coated in the sticky evidence of Steve's satisfaction. He slammed back, his hips bucking and rolling until Clint broke. He slammed forward with a whimper, his cock twitching, his whole body jerking, every nerve-ending flaring, and his heart hammering like war drums in his ears.

Clint didn't want to lose Steve's heat, so he let his softening cock remain buried inside his channel, falling on his back and curling around him, spooning him tighter than he ever held any girl.

"Can we do that again?" Steve asked sleepily.

"Absolutely. I think we can both agree we should do that many, many more times."

"Good. Do you have to work or anything tomorrow?"

"No."

"Good." Steve pulled the blanket over them and snuggled in closer. "I've been too nervous to sleep for the past week, so I'm going to get some shut eye."

"Nervous over what?"

Steve sniffed. "Isn't that obvious? You."

It wasn't obvious, but Clint would accept that answer. He ghosted his lips over Steve's temple, holding off his own exhaustion until the man in his arms fell asleep.

8 DOUBLE BIRTHDAY PLEASURE

Penn, a porn model and escort, is summoned to a casino in California for a very special birthday party. The birthday boy has always been fascinated by the idea of double penetration, and he wants an ass that can take two cocks. Penn's perfect for the job, and he does everything he can to make the birthday dreams come true.

Penn wasn't intimidated. Just because the man who summoned him to the Thunder Mountain Hotel and Casino happened to be the man who owned it, that was nothing to freak out over. Most of his clients were wealthy—it just so happens that Tony Storke was more wealthy than most and far more famous. Wealthy and famous enough that he could afford the absolute best. And by best, he meant discrete. Well, Penn could do discrete. He was like an undercover spy moving through the bedrooms of the most powerful men in the country, only he never used the intelligence he gathered. Maybe one day, he'd write a book, but in the meantime, he was happy to be the keeper of great (and terrible) secrets.

He received an envelope that morning containing a short page of instructions and a key to the pent house at the top of the casino. He avoided eye contact with the plain clothes security guards as he walked through the floor of the casino to the bank of elevators, but he did nod and smile at a few of the cocktail waitresses when they made eye contact with him. He felt a certain kinship with them. He caught an elevator just before the doors swished shut, cramming himself in with at least ten other people. They already reeked of booze, and they were carrying on five or six conversations between the ten of them, juggling responses and questions back and forth until the doors finally opened on the pool deck. Then he was left by himself.

The elevator took him all the way to the top floor where he had to use his key to open the door. He stepped into a private corridor and went directly to the door at the end of the hall, as his note instructed. A man he didn't recognize answered his soft knock, and Penn had to catch his breath. He couldn't remember the last time he felt a twinge of attraction for one of his clients, but this man was different. An unexpected work of art in a world of decay. His smile and eyes were pleasant—sincerely pleasant—and his brown hair sat in a mop of ringlets and curl on the top of his scalp. He had a faint five o'clock shadow, and his lips were full and pink. He had a drink in one hand, and he gestured Penn with the other, announcing, "Our guest has arrived" as he closed the door.

The man who hired him emerged from the next room, a drink in each hand. He crossed over in long strides and placed the cool glass against the palm of his hand. "Hello, Penn," he purred. "It's so good to see you again."

Penn blinked, surprised. To his knowledge, he never met Tony Storke face to face, but he also had no desire to contradict one of his clients. The first word he removed from his vocabulary once he became an escort was "No."

"You don't remember me, do you?"

"I'm afraid I don't. My apologies."

He chuckled. "Don't worry about it. You were rather distracted; I don't think you realized I was in the room. Bob Isla's party?"

Penn's eyes widened. "You were there?"

"Yes, of course. Why do you think I called you?" He put his arm around the other man's shoulders. "This young man is rather remarkable. He can take anything up the ass."

"Is that a fact?" He asked softly, brown eyes still locked on him.

"Yes. Would you like a practical demonstration?"

"Yes, I think I'd rather enjoy that."

"Your wish is my command." He directed Penn to the bedroom with his eyes. "After you, my friend."

He turned his back on them and made sure to give them a real show as he walked away. His ass was probably his most sought-after feature. People who liked bubble butts absolutely loved him. People who didn't care about the shape of the butt still found plenty of joy there. He loved to be fucked, plain and simple. He actually never met a bigger ass slut than himself, and if he ever did, he'd want to buy that man a coffee and shake his hand. Once he stepped into the bedroom, he undressed and crossed to the bed. He knew how to put himself on display, and when the other two men stepped into the room, he was on all fours, his ass proudly in the air.

"Do you model, too?"

"Oh you've definitely seen his movies, Bruce. I have a half dozen of them in my collection."

Bruce's lips twitched. "I had no idea you were such a fan."

"I told you tonight was going to be special, didn't I?" He yanked Bruce against him, his arm low around his waist. Bruce tilted his chin to catch the kiss Tony pressed to his mouth, their tongues sliding together. They kissed with a certain familiarity—they'd clearly done it many, many times before, but there was still a spark there, a real passion that Penn rarely saw anymore. He didn't make a sound; like a good prop, he patiently waited for them to emerge from the deep kiss and remember he was there.

They took turns undressing each other, murmuring softly to each other, occasionally chuckling, while the garments disappeared. When Bruce was naked, he sat on the mattress and held a straw up to Penn's lips. Penn eagerly drank down the offered drink, not realizing until he swallowed that he just took a giant gulp of gin.

"Easy there," Bruce said as he coughed and sputtered. "You okay?"

"Bit stronger than I expected."

"Yeah, it packs a punch, doesn't it?"

"Honey, where did you put the bag of supplies?"

"In the closet, sweetheart."

Penn had to admit that was pretty

damned cute. He also had to wonder just what was in Tony's "bag of supplies." He felt a lick of anticipation and another of excitement, and maybe there was a tiny tingle of fear, because there was always that little tingle at the very beginning, when he didn't know what he was getting himself into. He supposed when that went away, and he was completely numb to everything that happened he'd stop escorting and go back to his dull-day job at the tax firm.

"I'll take that," Bruce said. Penn looked over his shoulder to see he meant the lube. Tony had a velvet cloth spread at the top of the bed, onto which he put a series of butt plugs, each one bigger than the previous. By the time he pulled out the one as thick as his forearm, Penn's stomach was clenched tight, and his dick was hard. Clearly, Tony knew what his specialty was and where his talents were. That was fine with him. A man like Tony would see it as a challenge to break the ass that couldn't be broken, and Penn was all about rising to a challenge.

It started easy enough, with a butt plug no thicker than a man's finger. Penn greeted the insertion with a soft sigh, his cock jerking with the sensation of being filled. It felt good, and there was no resistance as Bruce fucked him with it. Soon, that disappeared, and there was one slightly thicker, which slipped in just as easy. Penn didn't really start to feel anything until the fourth plug, which was shaped like a short, fat dildo, designed to spread his hole. Bruce worked it in and out, twisting it with every stroke. Sometimes he moved slowly, sometimes he went fast, but he didn't stop until Penn stopped groaning and accepted the width silently.

That was the last time he was quiet again for a long, long time. There were ten total, and the sixth one was as thick as a small fist. He gripped the bedspread, forcing himself back every time he wanted to lunge forward to escape the hot sensation, the way the pain and the friction burned through him. His entire groin ached, his cock throbbing in time with the rapid beating of his heart. A hand buried in his hair and twisted, yanking his head back. He didn't expect Tony's slick, tequila-soaked mouth to land on his, the alcohol on his lips instantly absorbed into his bloodstream. He closed his eyes and moaned for more, and Tony's mouth disappeared to be replaced with the tequila bottle itself. The glass mouth kissed him, and tequila covered his tongue, his lips, his chin, and dripped down his neck. Tony poured more of the bottle over Penn's head for good measure, then set it aside and attacked him with his tongue. He licked the drops and streams away with rapid gestures and caught the rest with his lips.

He poured more of the bottle over the bridge of Penn's back, letting it tickle down his shoulders and ribs. Tony had more beard growth than Bruce, and the stubble scraped over his skin, stinging him where tequila made his skin wet. He made his way down Penn's body to where Bruce was currently forcing the seventh butt plug-in, spreading his already too-stretched ass out by less than a centimeter at a time, but taking every big of progress he could get.

"You know what's fascinating about tequila?" Tony asked conversationally.

"What?"

"It only takes a little bit...right here...to get you absolutely fucked up."

"Let's see."

He took in the sound of them kissing and then the splash of tequila coming down on his ass like fire. Every drop stung his tender and bruised skin, and Penn realized they were soaking the butt plug with it just seconds before Bruce pushed it forward, forcing the tip all the way to his bowels. The affects were instant, the room spinning and tilting around him, like a spinning top slowing to its unstable rest. He giggled because this was "funny." Everything was funny and rosy and flushed. His face tingled and went numb, and so did his ass. He couldn't feel the butt plug, just the pressure against his bruised walls.

"Do you think he's ready?" The question came from very far away.

"Close enough. I'm definitely ready."

"Mmm, I can tell. You feel magnificent. After you, sir."

Bruce stroked his dick, unable to take his eyes away from the whore's gaping asshole. He'd never stretched anybody out that far, and he knew he could push him even further, but his cock was hard and demanding that he replace the toys with something else. He'd always liked the thought of double penetration, and when Tony invited him out to California for his birthday and offered him the world, there was only one thing he really wanted to ask for. And Tony told him, "Is that all? That's easy. I even know the perfect person."

Turns out, the escort he called really was the perfect person. He was one of the prettiest boys Bruce had ever seen, the sort who is just unrelentingly attractive. No visible flaws or scars, no mars to distract from his beauty. His body was young and fit and tight, his muscles well developed. Not a single strand of his spiky blonde hair was out of place, and Bruce wondered if he wore contacts because he never saw eyes so blue in his life.

"What'll be the easiest way to do this?"

Tony tilted his head, considering the problem for only a moment before pointing at the mattress. "Get on your back. He can ride you, and then I can get him from behind."

"I like it."

Bruce obediently stretched out on his back, and the boy was so good he didn't need to be directly ordered to move. He straddled Bruce's body once the condom was in place. He didn't even need further urging to rock back. He took Bruce's thick cock in one easy stroke, and it was like sinking into the sweetest dream. He pulled Penn down by his shoulders until their chests were touching and invaded his mouth, kissing him passionately, chasing the faint taste of tequila on his tongue. He felt the mattress shift, and he broke away long enough to watch Tony over Penn's shoulder. He held Penn's shoulder, pulled him back, pushed him forward, pulling him back, made him rock faster and faster until he was panting and Bruce's face was twisted with too much pleasure.

"God, are you trying to make me cum?"

Tony huffed out a laugh. "No only making sure he's ready for this."

At first, Bruce couldn't feel a difference at all, though he knew Tony was lined up to entire Penn's stretched ring. He slid his crown up and down Bruce's shaft, and then pressed against Penn's muscle. Tony had a huge dick, and for a moment, Bruce wondered if he'd failed to stretch Penn enough. He absolutely didn't want to hurt the boy—well not too much. He didn't want to tear anything. He looked over to Penn's face, watching to see just how uncomfortable he was. It was difficult to tell, though, since he was moaning like a little slut, but his face was furrowed with distress, maybe even pain.

"You okay?" Bruce muttered.

Penn giggled. The sort of sound he only heard from drunks and small children.

Tony laughed. "I don't think he's with us anymore."

"Then what are you waiting for?"

"The good word." Tony pushed his hips forward, using enough force to drive his shaft into Penn's channel. Bruce shuddered as the thick length slowly slid over his throbbing flesh, the pressure becoming unreal, and the heat threatening to burn through him and leave him nothing more than a charred frame. Once Tony was inside, he took full control, using his hands on Penn's hips to hold him in place while he frantically thrust his own. He kept his strokes shallow quick, increasing the friction, increasing the burn.

"Oh fuck, Tony fuck...fuck...oh fucking fuck yes. Faster..." It was everything Bruce had hoped it would be when he made his request. It was even better than it looked when he watched it in porn. This was definitely not something he could walk away from and never try again. Hell, he didn't even think he could wait until the next special occasion. He didn't know what it was exactly, only that he'd never felt anything like this before in his life. "Oh fuck...I'm going to come...I have to..."

"Go ahead. We've paid up for the whole weekend. We'll be able to fuck him just like this as many times as you like."

The promise was the final push Bruce needed. He slammed his hips upward, pushing even deeper, eliciting a low man from Tony's throat as he shot into his condom. His cock wouldn't stop twitching, though, even after he emptied his sac, and Tony wouldn't stop moving, and the pleasure wouldn't stop rolling through him. He grabbed Penn by the back of the head again, claimed his mouth again, and screamed into his throat as he burst into another orgasm. Tony barely broke his stride, barely hesitated as he realized that Bruce was exploring the reality of male multiple orgasms.

"Oh fuck...fuck that's hot. God, Bruce."

"Come. I want to see you shoot all over him."

"Do you want me to shoot on his face? Hmm?"

"Yeah...yeah..."

Though he was sorry as soon as Tony pulled out of his ass. He missed the throbbing presence of his dick. Tony stood on the mattress over them, jerking himself off rapidly, his hips locked forward and his spine arched back. He dropped his head, gasped and swallowed, and then the white ropes exploded from him and hit Penn right in the face, rolling down his cheek and dripping from his nose. Bruce lost no time in cleaning it up, getting every last drop of it and the booze Tony had soaked Penn in earlier. A heady cocktail. Perfect for his birthday. Exactly what he wanted.

9 BUTTERFLY WING RHYTHM

Everybody noticed when he walked into the club. The air shifted, became electric with possibilities, and even the people who didn't know him--they did exist--sensed something had happened. They swung their heads around, watching as he approached the bar, the writhing, sweaty crowd parting before him, falling away like the Red Sea.

He didn't come out much anymore, and a question followed him through the packed club, a whisper of curiosity jumping from mouth to mouth like the air they were breathing. He heard it, of course, but he ignored it. He wasn't there for the masses, and he didn't have anything to say to them. His targets were sitting in the corner of the club, looking bored and watchful all at once, dressed in black, being perfectly conspicuous in their effort to remain out of sight. The man noticed him first, whispered something in the redhead's ear, and she quickly looked over, a smile playing across her fine features.

Eris walked up to their table without varying his stride, and the man nodded at the empty chair. As soon as he sat down, the waitress arrived with his favorite drink, setting it down in front of him with a bowl of lime and lemon wedges. He popped a yellow piece of fruit between his teeth and sucked the sour juice before taking a drink from the sweaty glass. The dancing resumed to normal once he was settled, and he smiled, waiting for them to break the silence. Lately he wasn't in any sort of mood to meet somebody new, but they both came very highly recommended. And he could see why. He didn't have a type--he found that far too limiting--but if he did, they would each be a perfect model. They were sexy and they knew it. Eris was intrigued.

"Would you like to dance?" She invited.

"I'd like to watch you two."

She stood, held out her hand to her partner, and he allowed her to pull him to his feet. They moved with easy grace, demanding attention with the way they walked, the way they slid together, the way they took up space. Once they were on the dance floor, they were almost inhuman. The music blared around them, the lights pulsing to the beat, and they were moving like they were inside of the music, like they were swimming in it. Watching a person dance could be very instructive, and watching these two move their hips in the rapid strobe lights told Eris everything he needed to know about what it would be like to take them to bed. They had perfect time, an innate rhythm, and a sense of trust that only came from a long partnership, one that saw both the good and the bad.

Eris took the time to finish his drink before standing. The dancers saw him approach and they held their collective breath. He took him by the hand first, yanking him against his body, their frames perfectly aligned. They moved their hips together, and she stood in front of him, her hands going to his hips, her full lips parting, and the tip of her tongue sticking out to tease him. They weren't in the middle of the floor, so the crowd re-arranged themselves, moving around the electric trio until they were dancing in the middle, surrounded by overheated bodies and the pure smell of sweat and adrenaline. The music changed, but it stayed the same, didn't disrupt them.

"What's your name?" Eris asked.

"Bart."

Eris didn't believe him, but it would do. "And hers?"

"Nat."

That wasn't a good enough name for her. It made Eris think of annoying bugs swarming at dusk. She deserved a better name. Something that rolled off his tongue as liquid and sweet as her body moved against his. He would rename her later, and when he was done with her, she would be more than happy to accept whatever name he gave to her.

They danced until Eris was slick with sweat and the beat was imprinted on his brain. They danced until they were panting and their hearts were beating and their skin was awake, alive to the entire stimulus around them. They danced until Eris's cock was hard and all he could think about was bending them over and taking his turn with each of their luscious asses. He took Bart by the wrist and Nat by the hand and pulled them to the back of the club. There was a door there that was marked No Entry, but signs like that never applied to him. They slipped into the darkened room and locked the door behind them. The walls shook and rumbled with the music, though they couldn't hear anything but the throbbing bass. The rest of the club was locked out, like they never existed.

Nat didn't stop dancing, though. She took a few steps back, ensuring each of them had the perfect view as she unzipped her leather halter. She took her time, slowly letting the teeth unlatch, gradually revealing her creamy skin. She spun around once the leather parted, showing the slopes of her shoulders. The halter fell away, revealing two butterfly tattoos, one red, and one yellow, on each shoulder blade. She was still moving, as slinky as a snake, her dance primal and older than time itself. She looked over her shoulder, her hair falling over one eye, a come-hither look in the other.

Bart wrapped his arms around her and spun her around. He put his mouth to her ear, murmured something, and she unzipped her skirt, showing him the world. The skirt fell down her hips and she kicked it off the pointed toe of her leather boot. She was completely smooth from the neck down, every inch of her calling for his mouth. Bart caught her arms and held them behind her back.

Eris advanced like a panther, his smile predatory, more of a bearing of teeth. Anybody else might have quaked a little bit, but this girl, this Nat, boldly met his eyes, the action almost a challenge. He couldn't remember the last time somebody challenged him, and desire like hot lava pooled in his lower stomach. He cupped both her breasts, squeezed, lifted them against his palm, and tested their weight. He squeezed harder and harder, watching her face for any reaction at all, but she kept her features impassive. He twisted his wrist, using enough pressure to make her bruise, and she finally gasped. He slid his fingers over each globe until he was only touching her nipples. He pinched the hard pebbles of flesh between his fingertips and his thumb. A hard pinch, a torque of his wrists, and she cried out, her knees bending. She would have dropped to the floor, but Bart held her up, easily bearing her weight.

Her face twisted with pain. He pinched harder. Her cry was louder, nearly a shout, and a shiver of satisfaction worked down his spine. He released her, allowing only a half second of relief before slapping each of her breasts, hard enough that the crack filled the room, overwhelming the music. A red handprint instantly bloomed across her creamy skin, and he did it again and again, the marks becoming welts. She moaned and thrashed, but she couldn't get away, couldn't escape the blows he rained down on her flesh.

He stopped as suddenly as he began, clutching her tits between his fingers and massaging and kneading them. Her cries of pain turned to moans of pleasure and she dropped her head back to her partner's shoulder. He could smell her and when he dragged his hand down her body he wasn't surprised to find a pool of arousal between her legs. He wasn't touching her for her benefit or pleasure, but knowing that she was turned on did make his dick all the harder.

"Do you want me to fuck you? Is that what you came here for?"

Her answer was a moan, so he grabbed her by the chin and forced her to meet his hard stare. "I asked you a question. Didn't you hear me?"

"Yes, sir."

"Call me Lover."

"Yes, Lover."

"Now do you want me to fuck you, little girl?"

"Yes, Lover."

"What's the magic word?"

"Please, Lover. Please fuck me."

Eris smiled and stepped back, hands going to his fly. He watched their expressions as he stripped, his smile widening when they finally got a look at his dick. Everybody knew he was big, but nobody ever believed the rumors, especially since they sounded more like exaggerated tall-tales or wishful thinking. But all of the rumors were quite true, and he was happy to prove it to anybody who asked nicely. Bart had asked quite nicely by bringing him the proper tribute, and he had no doubt that this was ultimately his idea. Or maybe he was being a good little pet who found the perfect dick for his mommy. Eris liked it, either way.

He took her by the arm and yanked her away from Bart, pulling her back against his groin. She trembled against him, like a leaf shaking in the wind, his cock sliding between her thighs, against her soft lips. He slicked his shaft with her sticky juices, pumped his hips back and forth to enjoy the feel of her swollen labia. She squirmed back against him, and she felt as electric as she looked, sparking, making him burn with lust.

He spun around and pushed her flush against the door, holding her there with one hand on his shoulder. The vibrations passed through the wood and into her body, and he could feel her thrumming with the insistent bass. He snapped his fingers and gestured Bart over, who quickly complied. He didn't need words to convey his desires, and Bart dropped to his knees beside them, ducking his head and angling his mouth to get a taste of where their flesh met.

His tongue was hot and slow like sticky syrup, slowly moving up and down his long shaft. He licked and mouthed and chased the flavor of Nat's desire before turning his attention to her silky skin. His tongue wiggled over her clit, pulling a new series of moans from her throat. Eris angled his cock towards her slit and took her without further ado, slamming his full length into her unresisting body. He could feel Bart's hot breath and slippery tongue everywhere she wasn't surrounding him, and he pumped his hips to the rhythm, throbbing like a heartbeat through her flesh.

It was better than she ever could imagine. Her hopes had been high after hearing the stories and the rumors, but in the back of her mind she always knew that he might not live up to them. But she could see that he would from the moment he walked into the club. There was a certain energy about him. He made the air buzz with electricity, and she could feel the heaviness, the power, of his gaze as it roamed over her body.

His cock was huge, but she firmly believed that what mattered was how he used it, not the size. Fortunately, he knew very well how to handle his weapon. His strokes were hard and measured and every second brought her untold pleasures. She pushed back against his heavy stroke, meeting him with enough force to make her teeth clack together. They were both grunting, not the most dignified sounds in the world, and every now and then she felt the whisper of Bart's tongue, or his breath, or the catch of his teeth on her tender skin. She widened her legs so he could fit his head between her thighs. He closed his lips around her clit and she bent her knees, pushing down to grinding against his mouth and then popping back to meet Eris's hard thrusts.

The pleasure was so intense that it was almost surreal. She felt like she was taking energy from the entire club and directing it with the flow of her body. Or maybe he was taking the energy, harnessing it, guiding it through her midsection so it would flow up and down her frame. Maybe that was the secret to his power. Her heart beat was the bass, her breath was the air tinged with sweat and pheromones, and her pleasure was climbing and climbing and climbing, pulling her spine as taut as a bowstring.

Bart gripped her thighs and Eris held her hips, and she felt like she was falling even though she'd never been held so tightly, never been so secure. Her hand closed into a fist and she banged against the door, hammering the wood and screaming every time he filled her. Nobody outside the door noticed, though, since it all blended into the music, her sounds melting into the backbeat.

Bart's mouth was watering, and his face was slick with sweat and pre-come and her juices. The taste on his tongue was a heady combination of sweat and sweet and salt and musk. The joining of Eris and Nat's bodies created a completely unique taste, a special experience that nobody will ever know but him. He swallowed it all down like it was the finest of wine, and he burned for more, burned to be completely surrounded.

He couldn't keep his tongue in one place. He played with her clit, and then went to her opening so he could hold his tongue against Eris's shaft as it slammed in and out of her. Every time he slid out, he was covered with fresh juices that smeared over Bart's mouth. His heavy balls hit Bart in the face more than once, and he caught them between his lips, sucking hard until he heard a deeper moan.

He knew people who came to this club, who played with Eris, and they always spoke of him in the most revenant tones. Like he was some sort of God on earth and they didn't want him to hear them use anything less than absolute respect. Bart wasn't so sure about that until Nat reached her first orgasm—and strangely enough it was to be her only orgasm. Because Eris would not let it stop. Bart followed his lead, licking and sucking on her clit as long as he pounded into her, and the pleasure kept coming and coming. He could feel it in the way she trembled and her clit jerked against his tongue with rapid pulses, like a butterfly wing flapping in his mouth.

The music stopped. She stopped. Everything froze except the rapid pounding of his heart. His hand automatically went to his cock and he closed his fingers around the shaft just as the music started again—louder this time. Harder. Pushing them faster and faster. Eris was a slave to the music and it guided every pump of his hips. Bart touched himself in the same rhythm, imagining his fist was Nat's pussy with each stroke.

She screamed, she bucked, she flailed, and she pleaded. Eris would not relent. He was not going to stop until he had his fill, even if she was like a raw and broken nerve. But then Eris moaned, "Fuck, I'm almost there."

Bart was really only one the floor between their legs for one reason. He knew Eris took her without a condom on, and so he yanked the giant dick from her pussy and closed his mouth around the flesh, taking him all the way down to the back of his throat. He cupped Eris's balls, squeezed as he swallowed, and triggered a tidal wave of cum. It flowed down the back of his throat in spurt after spurt. It was the sound of Eris's orgasm that set Bart off, though, ringing through his ears, echoing through his head, better than any music he'd heard that night.

His own orgasm whipped through him, fast and hot and stinging. He shattered with the force, shooting his load with enough force to send it across the room.

"That's a good start," Eris rasped, his voice deep and dangerous. "A very good start. Let's see what other fun games you two know."

Nat answered for both of them with her moan of approval.

10 THE LATE NIGHT RIDE

The only girl in a gang of men, Sarah is nothing more than a possession to serve them. But when that gang showed up on Tom's ranch, he could instantly see she's worth so much more than anything else. He offers her what he can without asking anything in return, giving her a late night ride she won't forget.

They rode in just after dusk, five in all. Tom greeted them in the yard, his gun strapped to his hip. Visitors weren't uncommon, but he couldn't be too careful, as close as he was to the Mexican border and as dry as the summer season was. Men had killed for a lot less than water, especially when it was rare as gold. He narrowed his eyes against the orange glare, picking out what details he could. There seemed to be four grown men riding in pairs, a lone boy between them on a smaller horse. They rode at a sedate pace, and Tom had plenty of time to prepare his greeting.

"Howdy."

The leader leaned off his horse and spat before nodding and flashing a rather amiable smile. "Howdy. Mind if we refresh ourselves?"

"You're welcome to have a drink. The well's around back."

"Jake?" The man to the left nodded at the boy.

"Right. Mind if we bunk down here tonight? We trapped our own varmints."

Tom nodded. "You can sleep in the barn." It wasn't the first time travelers had settled in for the night, but usually, they were deputized posses or Texas Rangers, either chasing somebody to the border or hauling somebody back from Mexico (rarer, the men they chased rarely came back alive). "Let me show you."

"Much obliged."

They rode to the barn and dismounted one by one. Their horses dropped their heads to sniff the ground, but there wasn't any grass for them. The boy fetched two buckets and filled them for the horses before pausing to take his own drink. He worked with his head down; his narrow shoulders slumped under the weight. He made two trips to ensure each horse got a drink, patiently stroking their cheeks while they slopped their mouths in the water. His horse drank last, and it turned its dripping muzzle to nuzzle his head, knocking his hat off in the process. And Tom saw that he was actually a she with strawberry blond hair and a dirty, pretty face. She laughed at the horse and pushed his head away, the sound as sweet as water in the desert, but it was cut off with a gruff, "Get these varmints taken care of girl."

There were three rabbits and a possum. A pretty good catch. He had a hard time imagining these four huge men scampering off rodents, so Tom expected it was the girl who tracked and trapped them. She quietly grabbed the rope from the back of her saddle they dangled from and moved away from the men gathered at the well.

"Shouldn't somebody help her?" Tom asked.

"No, she can do it."

"It might be faster if I..."

"I said she can do it," Jake said in a tone that wouldn't accept argument. Tom didn't take kindly to strangers telling him what to do on his own land, but he didn't want to start a quarrel with them. He was armed, but so were they, and he didn't like the odds of four against one.

"Where you boys heading?"

Jake turned hard eyes on Tom. "South."

He knew better than to press. Morning couldn't come quick enough. He didn't much like this Jake, and he didn't want to see his face longer than he had to.

Dinner was a quiet affair. Tom added sourdough biscuits and beans to the feast, and they all ate well. Except the nameless girl, who quietly waited until Jake and his men finished their meals before poking through the bones. She couldn't have found more than a few mouthfuls of meat on the carcasses and not much remained of the biscuits either. She went to see to the horses as they bedded down, and Tom excused himself, watching from his bedroom window to see what she did.

Sure enough, she slipped from the barn and scurried across the yard, a thin shadow beneath the sliver of moon. She poked around where they ate, looking for scraps like a dog, and Tom was so full of rage and sorrow that his hand automatically went to where his gun should be. He forced himself to take a deep breath and went to meet her with a plate of beans, biscuits, and bacon.

"Girl."

She froze.

"Come here."

She didn't move.

"Come here. I'm not going to hurt you. Look. I've got food."

She came to him, staring up at him with surprised, thankful eyes before accepting the plate. He ushered her inside the house, closing the door against the night and any spying eyes. He wasn't sure what would happen if Jake caught his girl sneaking around, but he didn't think the reaction would be a measured one.

"What's your name?" Tom asked, once she devoured her beans.

"Sarah. But no one calls me that anymore."

"Who's Jake? Your husband? Your pa?"

She shook her head. "He bought me from my pa."

"He bought you?"

"Yeah. Been riding with him ever since."

"Why don't you leave?"

"Leave where? He'll just track me down." She lifted her gaze to his. "And he'll kill any man who tries to help me. He says he bought me fair and square, and nobody's going to be taking me away."

"You can't stay with him. He'll kill you anyway."

"I don't have many options. Thank you

for the dinner. What would you like?"

"What would I like? Do you mean as payment?" Tom shook his head. "Payment isn't necessary. You should have enough food to eat."

"I can't repay the food. I'd like to repay the kindness." She stood and closed the distance between them. She stood toe to toe with him, and she was even smaller than he thought. She really was just a slip of a thing. "You can do whatever you like to   me."

"I...I don't want to do anything to you. Really. You should go get some sleep while you can. You'll need your rest."

"I'm not tired. If you won't let me do something for you, can I ask you to do something for me?"

"What's that?"

She took his hand and brought his palm to her cheek. She nuzzled against his hand, but he didn't respond, didn't curve his fingers against her cheek. "Touch me with something other than meanness."

He knew this was not a good idea. His brain was telling him that while his body reminded him that he hadn't touched anybody in a very, very long time. She was the first woman he'd seen in nearly a year, and it had been over two since he touched soft skin and found solace in welcoming arms. His fingers moved, and he cupped her face, holding her tiny head between his palms. She wrapped her fingers around his wrists and stared up at him with soft blue eyes. He dipped his head and let their mouths touch. Her lips were chapped and his were dry, but it was still nice—far nicer than anything else he'd ever experienced. His head flooded with possibilities, drowning out his concerns completely.

"I'll lock up." He released her, nodding at the loft. "The bed is up there."

He locked the door and put out the lamps, double checking to be sure all was still and quiet outside. When he was satisfied that Jake wasn't going to storm across the yard to shoot him in the head, he pulled his make-shift curtains closed and climbed up to the loft. She lay in the middle of his bed, and though it was perfectly adequate for him, it seemed too small for the two of them. He could tell she was naked, though he could barely see her. There wasn't any light coming through the window, and he didn't dare light a candle. He undressed himself quickly, wanting to be as naked as she was. Nothing should be between their skin. It was risky enough that he at least wanted to feel all he could for as long as possible.

He leaned over the bed, and she pulled him down to meet her, limbs folding around him, holding him with gossamer strength. She wasn't exactly soft—she was bony and wiry in turn, her slim body not allowed enough food to have any real curves. But her skin was smooth, and she kissed him with real interest, her tongue not the least bit shy as their kisses deepened. Her hands roamed up and down his back, alternating between the faint sting of her nails and a soothing caress. His muscles jumped everywhere she touched him, and he couldn't believe how much he enjoyed it. Or maybe he could. He couldn't remember the last time anybody touched him like that. Even the whores he occasionally visited usually kept their hands to themselves.

Tom moved away from her mouth, excitedly kissing her throat and neck. She used some of her water to wash the dirt away from her face and throat, but she still tasted like the trail and hard traveling. He inhaled and he smelled the sun and desert on her skin. He buried his face in her hair and smelled the wind blowing down from endless blue skies. He kissed her jawline, and over the bridge of her nose and the soft, fleshy part of her ears. He touched her without meanness, as she requested, his hands gentle, though he feared his skin was too roughened to feel that great. They're dry and calloused, his skin cracked across his fingers. He used the softer tips of his fingers, careful not to apply to much pressure while he explored her ribs and hips, her thighs and stomach.

She spread her legs wider and whimpered a small plea. His prick was already stiff, but the wanton invitation made him hard enough to pound nails. His head brushed across the soft skin of her inner thigh, and his rod jerked with anticipation of even softer skin. He wrapped his arms around her and rolled them over, putting her on his chest.

"Have you ever been on top?" He whispered.

"No."

"You do what you want."

"I want to feel your prick." She repositioned herself, gripping his shaft to guide the tip to her opening. Her heat whispered over his slick skin, and she was pressing down on him but not moving. It was all he could do not to slam his hips up to impale her. He told her he wanted her to do what she wanted, but his patience was nearly shot.

"Just push back, sweetheart."

"Like this?" She slammed back, and he

nearly yowled loud enough to wake the whole county. He bit down against the sound, pulling her down so he could bury his face against her neck. She clenched around him, fluttering and whimpering while she adjusted to the way he stretched her. He couldn't get a good grip on her, his hands moving up and down her body, his fingers trembling every time he touched her.

"Move...please...I..."

She obeyed, rocking so slowly she was barely moving at all. Still, that was better than the impossible, solid pressure when she did nothing but hold him deep and remain still. They had to keep it slow and quiet, had to bite back their moans and swallow down their shouts. She was good. She was so good she was killing him, and a greedy voice told him he should keep her. Maybe he could buy her himself. He had a few things of value hidden around his spread, and he would trade any of it for more of this, for more of her.

She pulled away from his embrace, straightening her spine and sitting up. He bent his knees behind her, bracing himself for the new angle and the new force. She took his hands, fingers lacing through his, and moved with an experimental bounce. The bed creaked beneath him as she landed on him, the sound becoming a steady accompaniment as she found her rhythm. He'd been happy to let her have this position, but he didn't expect to quite like it so much. It wasn't just the way her flesh closed around him; it wasn't just the friction, or the novelty of her body coming down on his. It was the combination of all three and more, the undefinable spark of her passion, her joyful energy, and her regular, soft grunts.

She rode him most of the night, rode him until he broke, and then used her hands and mouth to make him hard again. When she finally collapsed on top of him, they were both weak and exhausted, slick with sweat and shaking from the aftershocks. He knew she had to leave, but he wrapped his arms around her, turning to his side and holding her against him, half trapping her between his body and the mattress.

She woke him before dawn with warm kisses across his grizzled jaw and turned into her mouth, tongue dipping between her lips. It was surprisingly easy to slide into her again, their bodies fitting together perfectly, but this time, he moved over her, watching her lovely face as the sun dipped through the cracks in the ceiling. He knew they didn't have a lot of time, and he kissed her sleepiness away, gradually amping up his tempo until he was plowing into her and she was rising to meet each hard thrust.

"Faster," she urged. "Faster. They'll be awake soon."

He nodded, the knowledge weighing heavy on him. After a night with her, he doesn't want to face a lifetime of nights alone. He slept better with her curled against him, and waking up to a warm body and a smile beat waking up to nothing but an unforgiving sun and endless work. Those things still existed, but she was like a buffer. More than the thought of being alone, he hated the thought of her being at the mercy of four brutes.

"I want you to say," he blurted.

"I can't."

"I'll buy you."

"He won't let you."

"I'll kill him."

"He's fast. They're all fast."

He stopped and stared down at her. "Do you want to stay with me?"

"I...yes. Of course I do."

"Then let's figure something out."

"I don't know how."

He fell into silence, and she shifted her hips, urging him to move again. He tried, but he couldn't withstand the motion, and they worked their way back up to a hard, pounding rhythm. Their mouths slammed together, and they kissed until the urge to scream had passed, and they were panting and exhausted once again. This time, he couldn't roll her over and fall asleep. He had to stand and try to clean himself off while she got dressed.

"Don't say anything today," she instructed before they left the loft.

"Today?"

"Just don't say anything. I can run away. Pete is supposed to have third watch, but he always makes me do it."

"But you said they'll just track you down."

"It'll give you a full day to prepare for them. And I can shoot."

"What if you don't come back?"

She stood on her toes to kiss his cheek. "I will be back."

Her words echoed in his head as he watched the group ride away, once again with two in front and two behind her. His hand went to his gun, and he considered shooting them in the back of their heads, but he wasn't fast enough to take all four of them out without returning fire. He could only hope that she would make good on her promise.

AUTHOR'S NOTE

Readers: I want to expand a few of the stories to see where the characters can be explored further. If there are any of the stories that you would like to read more about again, I'd love to hear from you!

Visit my blog at http://www.kelliegranier.com

Join my newsletter for free exclusive previews
http://www.kelliegranier.com/in

Follow me on Twitter at
http://www.twitter.com/kelliegranier

Like my page on Facebook at
http://www.facebook.com/kelliegranier

Discover my books at major ebook retailers everywhere.